Unfortunately
Average

Victoria Torres, Unfortunately Average
is published by Stone Arch Books,
A Capstone Imprint
1710 Roe Crest Drive
North Mankato, Minnesota 56003
www.mycapstone.com

Copyright © 2017 Stone Arch Books

Library of Congress Cataloging-in-Publication Data
Names: Bowe, Julie, 1962- author. | Bowe, Julie, 1962- Victoria Torres, unfortunately
   average.
Title: Dance fever / by Julie Bowe.
Description: North Mankato, Minnesota: Stone Arch Books, a Capstone imprint, [2017] |
   Series: Victoria Torres, unfortunately average | Summary: The Middleton Middle School
   fund-raising committee is looking for a theme for this year's event, and bossy Annelise
   insists on a formal dance, which her father will support with publicity and prizes, but the
   trouble is none of the boys want to come — so it is up to Victoria to get Annelise to
   agree to a compromise.
Identifiers: LCCN 2016032902| ISBN 9781496538192 (library binding) | ISBN
   9781496538215 (pbk.) | ISBN 9781496538277 (ebook (pdf))
Subjects: LCSH: Hispanic American children—Juvenile fiction. | Money-making projects
   for children—Juvenile fiction. | Dance parties—Juvenile fiction. | Middle-born
   children—Juvenile fiction. | Middle schools—Juvenile fiction. | CYAC: Hispanic
   Americans—Fiction. | Fundraising—Fiction. | Dance parties—Fiction. | Middle-born
   children—Fiction. | Middle schools—Fiction. | Schools—Fiction.
Classification: LCC PZ7.B671943 Dan 2017 | DDC 813.6 [Fic]—dc23
LC record available at https://lccn.loc.gov/2016032902

Designer: Bobbie Nuytten
Image credits: Photographs by Shutterstock: Hong Yo, 156 (popcorn), Michael Kraus,
cover (boots), Mike Flippo, cover (cowboy hat), Sfocato, cover (hay), Stanislav Khokholkov,
cover (Mexican hat); Line drawings by Capstone: Sandra D'Antonio and Shutterstock

Printed and bound in Canada.
10048S17FR

DANCE FEVER

by Julie Bowe

STONE ARCH BOOKS
a capstone imprint

All About Me

Hi, I'm Victoria Torres — Vicka for short. Not that I am short. Or tall. I'm right in the middle, otherwise known as "average height for my age." I'm almost twelve years old and just started sixth grade at Middleton Middle School. My older sister, Sofia, is an eighth grader. My little brother, Lucas, is in kindergarten, so that puts me in the middle of my family too:

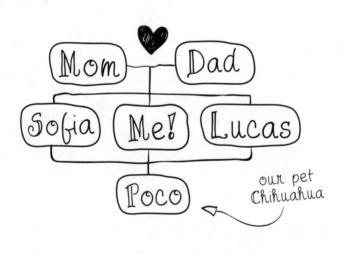

our pet Chihuahua

I'm average in other ways too. I live in a middle-sized house at the center of an average town. I get Bs for grades, sit in the middle of the flute section in band, and can hit a baseball only as far as the shortstop. And even though she would say I'm "above average," I'm not always the BEST best friend to my BFF, Bea.

Still, my parents did name me Victoria — as in victory? They had high hopes for me right from the start! This year, I am determined to be better than average in every way!

 Me!

Chapter 1

The Perfect Plan

"Dig in, dudes," our class president, Henry, says. He waves a bag of pretzels as he walks into the Middleton Middle School library for our fund-raising committee meeting after school.

Henry, Annelise, Sam, and I are here, repping the sixth-grade class. There are seventh and eighth graders on the committee too, including my sister, Sofia. She's our chairperson. We've met a couple times. Last week Sofia asked Henry to bring snacks to this meeting.

Annelise wrinkles her nose, looking at the bag of pretzels Henry just tossed onto the table. It's crumpled and half empty. Henry must have gotten hungry during school today!

"That's *it*?" Annelise complains. "Couldn't you have baked some brownies or bought a box of donuts, at least? When it was *my* turn to bring snacks, *I* served carrot and celery sticks with homemade hummus dip."

"Don't remind us," Sam says, making bunny ears over Annelise's head. "We're all trying to forget that rabbit food."

Henry snickers and pulls up a chair, cowboy style, next to Sam. He pops a fistful of pretzels into his mouth, then passes the bag around.

Annelise wrinkles her nose all the way up to her perfectly plucked eyebrows. But she snags some pretzels from the bag before they're all gone.

"Never mind about the snacks," Sofia says, picking up a marker that sits on a whiteboard next to our table. "We have more important things to discuss. Principal Oates wants us to nail down a theme for our fund-raiser so we can start working on pub-licity. Remember, this will be our school's biggest moneymaker of the year. The teachers and PTO will help our parents with the food and decorations, but it's our job to get students and families excited about coming to the event. If we plan it right, this could be the best fund-raiser in the history of Middleton Middle School!"

Each year our school puts on a community-wide fund-raiser. Usually, there are carnival games, a food booth, and activities during the day, followed by a dance for students in the evening.

Last year the committee went with a fifties theme. Everyone dressed up in poodle skirts, white T-shirts, cuffed-up jeans, and letter jackets. Girls wore high ponytails and guys slicked back their hair. The parents set up the parking lot like a drive-in restaurant, and there was even a mock drag race on the football field with kids my age riding tricycles! It was super fun. For the dance that night, they held a sock hop.

I wasn't in middle school last year, but Sofia said some of the teachers taught the kids how to do dances called The Bunny Hop and The Twist! The money they raised helped pay for new tables and benches in our school's courtyard, plus a ramp for the skateboard park in town. This year, we're raising money to buy new laptops for the school's library.

"I say we skip the dance this year and have a concert instead!" a seventh-grade girl named Laksha suggests.

Henry does fist pumps above his head. "Now we're talkin'!" he says. "Like a rock concert! That would totally . . . er . . . rock! We could hire some big-name band from the city. Pack the gym!"

Sofia rolls her eyes. "We can't afford to bring in a real rock band," she says. "Remember, we have to pay for the event through donations and ticket sales."

Henry slumps. So does Laksha.

"Everybody likes pizza," says Sam. "We sold them for Scouts and made a lot of dough."

"Pizza dough?" Henry jokes.

Sam laughs. "*Green* dough." He rubs his fingers together like he has dollar signs in his eyes.

"I like the idea of serving pizza, but we need other things going on too," Sofia says. "Games for the little kids, different kinds of food that everyone will like, and some sort of dance for all the middle school students."

Annelise stands up, flicks back her long hair, and marches up to the whiteboard where Sofia is standing.

"I have a fantabulous idea to share," Annelise says, holding out her hand for Sofia's marker. "I've been waiting very patiently to tell everyone about it because it's the *best* idea."

Sofia frowns, but she gives the marker to Annelise. Annelise smiles and motions for Sofia to take a chair.

Reluctantly, Sofia sits down. Sometimes it's easiest to let Annelise have her way. She can be super bossy.

Turning to the board, Annelise starts writing in big, fancy letters.

"A formal what?" Henry asks, as Annelise adds flowers and curlicues around the word she's written.

"A formal *dance!*" Annelise replies, underlining her artwork with a flourish. "Think *Cinderella*. All the girls will dress in fancy gowns. All the guys will wear suits and ties. Instead of messy pizza, we'll serve finger sandwiches and punch! I told my dad all about my great idea last night. He loves it, of course, and has already offered to provide *all* the publicity — posters, tickets, fliers. He'll even get us cool swag to sell ahead of time, like tiaras for the girls and bow ties for the guys!"

Annelise's dad owns a big ad agency in the city, so he can make really cool posters and stuff at his office.

Henry's eyes go wide. "You want *me* to wear a tie?" He shudders like Annelise just suggested he swap his wrestling T-shirt for a straight jacket. "No way. Count me out!"

Sam nods in agreement. So does Alex, an eighth-grade boy. The only boy who doesn't seem to mind Annelise's plan is a quiet seventh grader named Will. But he's already wearing a tie!

"I'm okay with a dance," Sam says, "but does it have to be a formal? Like Sofia said, we should plan a fund-raiser the whole school will like. Why not get a local DJ to spin some tunes so we can dance like crazy?"

I perk up at this idea. A DJ dance sounds like a lot more fun than a fancy formal. Annelise likes to do everything with a lot of sparkle and style. I like to sparkle too, but I've got my own style. I'd rather dance around with my friends than worry about tripping over a frilly dress or waltzing on my dance partner's toes! Unfortunately, disagreeing with Annelise can get a person into *trouble*. I've worked on projects with her before. She is never happy unless she's calling the shots.

Right on cue, Annelise crosses her arms and scowls. "My dad agreed to support a *formal*, not a kiddie dance."

The boys start grumbling again about wearing suits and ties. Laksha and a couple other girls start whispering about mosh pits and rock bands.

Sofia bites her lip nervously. She's probably watching her goal of having the number-one fund-raiser in the history of our school fizzle before her eyes! Sofia can be as bossy as Annelise sometimes, but she *is* my sister. I don't want her goal to fail. And Annelise's dad is making a generous offer. It would be silly not to find a way to keep everyone happy.

"Couldn't we choose a theme that's somewhere in the middle?" I blurt out.

Everyone stops talking and looks at me. *¡Uf!* I'm not used to being the center of attention. Except for Will, I'm the quietest member of our committee. My cheeks begin to blush.

Laksha leans toward me. "Like what, Vicka?"

"Yeah, Vicka, what have you got in mind?" Henry asks. "Anything's gotta be better than neckties and Tinkerbelle crowns."

Annelise crosses her arms harder and squints at me. "This had better be good, Vicka."

I gulp, thinking for a moment. "We're studying the Wild West in history class this quarter. Instead of dressing up in suits and gowns, how about we dress up in Western costumes, instead? You know, cowboy boots and jeans? The girls could still wear dresses if they want. Instead of selling tiaras and bowties, we could sell cowboy hats for everyone to wear . . . maybe in our school colors?"

"Hey, that's a great idea!" Sofia exclaims.

I smile, happy that my sister agrees with me for once!

Henry nods. "We can make the whole thing one big Wild West show! We'll turn the concession stand in the gym lobby into a chuck wagon and serve up cowboy grub, like hot dogs and cactus juice punch! Get a DJ to spin some country tunes for the dance. Heck, we could even have a dunk tank! Call it the Waterin' Hole and give the teachers a good, long drink!"

Everyone loves that idea! I mean, who doesn't want to soak their favorite teacher?!

"My grandparents own a farm," Alex says. "I could ask them to give people hayrides around the football field. Maybe they'd even bring along some farm animals for the little kids to feed and pet." He grins. "We could ask Principal Oates to kiss a cow if we reach our fund-raising goal. That would bring in a truckload of money!"

We all start talking at once, getting more and more excited.

"*Hayrides*? Kissing *cows*?? Dunking *teachers*???" Annelise throws down her marker and punches her fists into her hips. "My dad agreed to tiaras and bow-ties, *not* cactus juice and cowboy hats! Besides, my mother is on the PTO. There's no way she will be in favor of a *barn* dance."

"I can guarantee none of the guys will come to a formal," Henry says. "We like Vicka's idea better."

Sam and Alex nod, sitting shoulder to shoulder with Henry.

"I like *my* idea," Annelise shoots back. "So do my parents."

"Calm down, everyone," Sofia says. "Fighting isn't going to help us make this the best fund-raiser ever. I'm sure we can work out our differences."

I sink down in my chair like it's turning into quicksand. The committee likes my idea, but Annelise doesn't. I'm stuck in the middle again. Unfortunately!

Chapter 2

A Ginormous Problem

After our meeting, Henry and Sam catch up to me in the hallway. "Wait up, Vicka," Henry says. "We need to talk to you, like, seriously."

"What is it?" I ask, glancing up at a clock on the wall. I'm supposed to meet my BFFs, Bea and Jenny, at our favorite hangout, Java Jane's. We're studying for a history test.

"You've got to talk some sense into Annelise," Sam says. "Get her to give up her dorky plan for a formal. None of the guys will come if we have to bring a date and dress up in penguin suits."

Henry nods in agreement. "We want our fund-raiser to be a hit. But if Annelise gets her way it's going to be a major flop. You've got to make her change her mind."

"Look, I don't want the dance to be formal, either," I say, "but you guys, I'm the last person Annelise will listen to."

"Not true," Henry replies. "She respects your opinions."

"Since when?" I ask.

Henry thinks for a moment. "Remember last week in study hall?" he asks. "Bea said green gummy bears tasted best, and you said purple gummy bears were way better. Annelise completely agreed with you."

I roll my eyes. "We were just joking around! And we were talking about candy flavors! This situation is different. Annelise is serious about having a formal. Once she makes up her mind about something, nothing and no one can change it. Especially not someone like me."

Mr. Hamilton, our custodian, pushes a cleaning cart past us. It's getting late. I glance at the clock again.

Sam gives my shoulder an encouraging pat. "Talk to her tomorrow, Vicka. We're counting on you! You're our only hope."

"Yeah," Henry adds, galloping toward the doors. "You're our only hope!"

"But . . ." I start to say.

Henry and Sam bolt outside, leaving me to deal with the problem on my own. *¡Uf!*

❀ ❀ ❀

When I finally get to Java Jane's, Bea and Jenny are working on their second round of hot chocolates, but they saved a cookie for me.

"How was your meeting?" Jenny asks, sliding the cookie plate toward me. I start telling them about our plans for the fund-raiser. "Everyone was super excited about my idea for a Wild West theme."

"Ooh!" Bea exclaims. "That does sound like fun! Remember when we had to learn square dancing in fifth grade? Now we can try out our do-si-do moves!" She crosses her arms and bounces on her chair.

"Yeah, but there's one ginormous problem," I say.

"What's that?" Jenny asks.

"Annelise wants the dance to be formal. You know, like Cinderella's ball? She already got her dad to agree to pay for all the publicity. Plus, her mom is on the PTO committee. She'll get her to vote against our Western theme."

"But, I'd rather wear jeans and a cowboy hat than a dress and heels," Jenny says.

I nod. "Other kids feel the same way. Henry and Sam want me to convince Annelise to change her mind," I say.

Jenny perks up. "Hey, that's a great idea!"

"Yeah!" Bea says. "That will fix everything!"

My jaw drops. "You two know Annelise won't agree to anything unless it's her idea."

Jenny does a sly smile. "Then you just have to bribe her a little," she says.

Bea nods. "Tell her we'll crown her queen of country if she agrees to the Wild West theme. She'll be so gaga over the idea of ruling the dance floor that she won't even care about the formal. And we'll get to have fun stomping around in cowboy boots!"

"That's genius, Bea," Jenny says. Then she turns to me. "See, Vicka? Problem solved."

Bea and Jenny start sipping hot chocolate again and quizzing each other on our history unit. But I push away my cookie and rest my head in my hands. I've lost my appetite. And my forehead feels hot, like I've got the flu. Is there such a thing as *dance fever*? If there is, I think I'm coming down with a serious case!

When I get home from Java Jane's, Sofia is waiting for me. The first words out of her mouth are, "Vicka, you have *got* to talk to Annelise!"

"*¡Ay!*" I exclaim. "First the boys, then my friends, and now you?" I shake off my backpack and start for the stairs, hoping I can hide in my bedroom. "Why does everyone think I can change her mind? I can barely change a lightbulb!"

Sofia follows me upstairs, ignoring my complaints as she continues to talk my ears off. "I met with Principal Oates after school, and she *loves* our idea of a Wild West theme! She already promised to talk to the PTO about paying for the dunk tank! Best of all, she said she will definitely kiss a cow if we reach our fund-raising goal! I bet we'll surpass it now! You have got to get Annelise to saddle up to our plan."

I stop outside my bedroom door and face my sister. "*You* are in charge of our fund-raising committee! It's your job to talk to her!"

Sofia shakes her head. "She won't listen to me. Let's face it, she wants my job. But you two are friends. She'll listen to you."

I laugh. "I'm barely her friend. And Annelise doesn't listen to anyone. Especially not an average girl like me."

I head into my bedroom. Sofia follows me. "If we don't get Annelise to agree to our plan, we'll lose her dad's support. His donation will help keep our expenses low. The more donations we get, the more money we will raise for our cause. Plus, getting all the publicity done by his ad agency will make our fund-raiser look really professional! No one will be able to resist coming to our event. We are sure to raise more money than any other committee in the history of Middleton Middle School!"

Sofia's eyes gleam like gold medals when she says that last part. There's nothing Sofia likes more than being number one at everything she does. In some ways, she and Annelise are a lot alike. They both crave to be the best, and they don't let anyone stand in the way of their goals.

I push my glasses up on my nose and give my sister a serious squint. "We're supposed to be raising money to help our school. But it sounds like you only care about making sure our fund-raiser is better than any other fund-raiser!"

Sofia purses her lips. "And what's wrong with wanting to be the best? It's what Mom and Dad are always telling us . . . 'Do your best!' They wouldn't want us to back down from a challenge. Families stick together and help each other, Vicka. Now I need your help to convince Annelise that our country dance will be better than her formal. Talk to her at school tomorrow and get her to agree to my . . . I mean, *our* plan!"

As much as I dread the idea of trying to convince Annelise to change her mind, I can't disagree with my sister's reasoning. Our family does stick together and help each other reach our goals — everything from helping Lucas learn his ABCs, to helping our grandmother, Abuela, grow the prettiest flower garden in her neighborhood.

It was easy to make excuses to Henry and Sam. I could even make excuses to Bea and Jenny. But Sofia is my sister. When she asks me to do something for her, no excuse is big enough. Being the number-one fund-raiser in the history of Middleton Middle School is Sofia's goal. If I help her succeed, I will shine with my family and with my school.

"Fine," I say with a sigh. "I'll talk to Annelise. But I doubt it will do much good."

Sofia smiles. "You'll think of something to get her on our side. Oh, and don't forget, we have another planning meeting at the end of the week. Make sure she's on board by then."

"No problem," I reply, even though it feels like a ginormous problem. I'd rather kiss a cow than try to get Annelise to take my side!

As soon as Sofia leaves, I click up Abuela's number on my phone. Our grandmother is always full of good advice. I'm hoping Abuela can help me figure out how to handle Annelise.

"*Hola*, Victoria!" Abuela says when she answers her phone a moment later. "I was just thinking about you!"

"You were?" I say, taking this as a positive sign. I've always felt a special bond with my grandmother because we share a birthday. Maybe Abuela is so tuned in to me, she already knows a quick solution to my problem!

"*Si*," Abuela replies. "I just bought a new box of flower bulbs for my garden! I was hoping you could stop by this weekend and help me plant them. Gardening is always more fun with you."

"Oh," I say, feeling a little disappointed. "Sure, Abuela, I'd love to lend a hand."

I can hear my grandmother smile into the phone. "*¡Gracias!* Now tell me what it is you're calling about. I have a feeling it's more important than planting flowers."

Starting at the beginning, I tell Abuela all about our fund-raising committee and our plans for a country dance to go along with our Western games, hayride, and cowboy food. "But one girl on our committee, Annelise, wants our dance to be formal with frilly dresses and fancy finger food instead," I explain. "It's not a bad idea; it's just that everyone else wants the dance to be more fun and casual. But Annelise refuses to agree and go along with the rest of us."

"Hmm," Abuela says. "Getting everyone to agree can be a real challenge."

"But that's not my main problem, exactly." I switch ears and continue. "My problem is that Sofia and my friends want *me* to talk to Annelise and get her to change her mind. Annelise, the most stubborn girl in our class! They seem to think I have some superpower over her. But I don't! I'm just me, Abuela. Victoria Torres, unfortunately average. I'm no superhero."

"You may not be a superhero," Abuela says, "but you do have a superpower, Victoria."

I blink with surprise behind my glasses. "I do?"

"*¡Si!* You are a super *friend*! You are a friend to me and to your family and to your classmates. I've seen you accept people as they are and help them even when you don't know how things will end."

"But, Abuela, it's different with Annelise. She isn't exactly my friend. And I know what she wants in the end — to get her own way and rule the world."

Abuela chuckles. "There must be a way you two can reach a compromise. Then everyone will win."

I sigh. "But what kind of compromise?"

"That I don't know," Abuela replies. "Talk with her about working together in a way that will make everyone happy. If you give a little, she might give a little too."

"Okay, Abuela," I reply, reluctantly. "I'll try to make a deal with Annelise, even though I'd rather work things out with a very hungry lion."

Abuela laughs. "That's my girl, Victoria! You might be surprised how easy it is to agree."

I thank Abuela for her help before I hang up the phone. Then I sigh to myself. Abuela doesn't know Annelise. With her, nothing is easy.

Chapter 3

Reaching a Compromise

When I get to school the next day, Annelise is already there, talking up her idea of having a formal for our fund-raiser. "My dad is even going to rent a limo for me and all of my friends!" Girls are buzzing around her with excitement, hanging on her every word. "There will be a red carpet to walk down! The gym will sparkle with a million tiny lights! The buffet table will be filled with ice sculptures, layer cakes, and platters of delicious finger sandwiches!"

"What are finger sandwiches, exactly?" Sam asks Henry and Drew as they throw their coats and backpacks into their lockers. My locker is close by, which makes me happy because I get to see Drew all the time. I've had a secret crush on him since the start of the school year.

Henry shakes his head, gravely. "You don't want to know, my friend." He wiggles his fingers at Sam.

Drew snickers. "I think it just means they're small enough to pick up with your fingers and pop into your mouth."

"That's what they want you to think, Drewster," Henry replies. "Trust me, stay as far away from *finger* sandwiches as you can!"

Drew and Sam laugh as Henry wiggles his fingers again. Then they give him head noogies as they head to class. I have to step out of the way quickly to avoid getting knocked over like a bowling pin.

"Oops!" Drew says as he bumps past me. "Sorry, Vicka! I didn't step on your toes, did I?"

"N-no, my toes are fine," I say, even though he did step on one of my feet. But I don't want my crush to feel bad about almost crushing my big toe!

"Your toes may be fine, but how are your *fingers*?" Henry asks me. "You've got to get Annelise to change her mind before someone loses a pinkie!"

"Did you talk to her yet?" Sam chimes in.

I shake my head. "Not yet," I reply.

Drew tosses me a smile. "The guys told me she's got issues with a Western theme. But I think it sounds like a hoot." He do-si-does with Sam. They all crack up, then take off down the hall again. "I know you'll get her to change her mind, Vicka!" Drew calls over his shoulder as they disappear around the corner.

I lean against my locker, rubbing my squashed foot. But as I limp off to class, there's a smile on my face. Drew likes my idea for a Wild West theme. He even thinks I can convince Annelise to agree with the committee. When your crush has confidence in you, it makes you feel like anything is possible!

By lunchtime, every clump of girls I pass in the hallways is chatting about limo rides and sparkly dresses. Why would Annelise agree to a compromise now? So many of her friends are already on her side.

Still, I go looking for Annelise. I may be an average girl, but I am *above* average in keeping my promises. I told Sofia I would try to change Annelise's mind. And Abuela is right. I *am* a good friend. Like she said, if I reason with Annelise in a friendly way, maybe everything will turn out all right. Right? *¡Uf!*

A few minutes later, I find Annelise standing in front of the mirrors in the girls' restroom, combing her perfectly combed hair. I step in next to her and start tucking my loose strands of hair behind my ears and consider the smudges on my glasses. Taking them off, I clean the lenses on the edge of my sweater, then put them on again and look at Annelise with pretend-surprise. "Oh, hi, Annelise, I didn't see you there!"

Annelise gives my reflection in the mirror a blank look. "I've been standing right here the whole time,

Vicka. Maybe you need new glasses? But never mind. Did you hear the great news about my dad renting a limo for our formal? It will be a total blast!"

I take a big breath, trying to muster up every ounce of confidence I have. "I wanted to talk with you about that," I say.

Annelise's comb pauses as she looks at my reflection again. "What about it?" she asks. "Oh, are you wondering if you can come for a limo ride too? I suppose I can try to squeeze you in."

"No," I reply. "But I think it's really nice of your dad to help us out in such a big way, with the publicity and everything. Except, the thing is, I . . . I mean, *we* . . . the committee . . . we really think a Wild West fund-raiser is the way to go." I turn to Annelise and give her arm a friendly squeeze. "Just think of it. Rhinestone hats and belts . . . frilly skirts and fringed vests . . . pink cowgirl boots! We could even crown *you* queen of the country!" I look squarely at Annelise. "We need *you*."

Annelise pulls a lip gloss from her pocket, unimpressed with my little speech. "It's a *dance*, Vicka, not a coronation. And the only reason you *need* me is so that my dad will pay for most of it." She leans into the mirror and puts on a fresh layer of gloss.

I bite my lip. "Okay, forget the queen thing. And, I admit, what you said about your dad is partly true. But we also want you on our side because you're part of our committee. If one person isn't happy, it makes everyone unhappy. And you are the best person to get people excited about an event like this. It took you only *one* day to get *fifty* girls excited about a limo ride. Getting people jazzed up is your thing, Annelise. It's like your . . . superpower."

Annelise wrinkles her brow. "What do you mean, my *superpower*?"

"You know, some people are good at basketball. Others are math aces. Some are musical prodigies. *Your* gift is getting people involved and excited to do big things."

Annelise blinks a few beats, like she isn't sure if I'm joking or serious. Then she smiles to herself. "I suppose you're right. I *am* good at getting people to go along with me."

I smile back. "If you would just agree to our Wild West theme, we could have the biggest, best fundraiser ever! Our committee will be working together, and you'll be in charge of making sure the whole school knows about the great dance we'll have at the end of the day!"

Annelise shifts her hips, thinking this through.

I hold my breath, waiting for her answer.

"You're right, Vicka," she finally says. "We *all* need to agree to the same plan."

I blink with surprise. "I'm right? Does that mean you will agree to our Wild West theme?" A glimmer of hope flickers in my chest.

Annelise nods. "Yes, I'll agree to everything . . . hayrides, hot dogs, a dunk tank . . . a barn dance. I'll even get my dad to help cover the cost."

I brighten. Abuela was right! This wasn't so hard after all!

"I only have one condition . . ." Annelise says, tucking away her lip gloss and comb.

My face freezes. "What?" I ask.

Annelise purses her glossy lips. "If the boys are too immature to dress up for a formal, then there's no way they will ask us girls for dates. That's why our dance will be a Sadie Hawkins."

I raise my eyebrows. "What's that?"

"It's a country dance, so everyone will still dress up like cowboys and cowgirls, but the *girls* have to invite the boys!"

I blink. "You mean . . . *I* have to ask a boy . . . to be my date?"

Annelise nods. "It's the perfect solution. The girls get to go with the boys they choose instead of waiting for the slowpoke boys to never ask them for a date." She smiles and squeezes my arm. "What do you say, Vicka? Deal?"

I hesitate for a moment. If I agree, we'll get lots of help paying for the fund-raiser. And Annelise won't have anything to complain about. Plus, if the girls ask the boys to the dance, then the boys will have to come. They all wanted us to think they had cooties in elementary school, but things are different in middle school. Now the boys want us to think they're cool.

I give Annelise a nod. "Okay," I say. "I agree. So will the committee."

Annelise pats my head like I'm her puppy. "I knew you'd come around to my way of thinking." As we head out of the restroom, she takes off for the Caf, stopping kids along the way. "Have you heard the news? Forget the formal. I've decided we're having a Sadie Hawkins dance instead!"

Annelise agreed to a compromise after all. We get our country theme, but now I have to ask a boy to the dance. Nothing is easy when you are unfortunately average!

Chapter 4

Hat Dance

At our fund-raising meeting on Friday, everyone is super excited about Annelise's suggestion for a Sadie Hawkins dance.

"There's only *one* problem with your plan, Annelise," Henry says, snagging a donut from the box Alex brought for a snack.

Annelise frowns. "What is it?"

Henry takes a bite of the donut, powdered sugar dusting his lips and the front of his wrestling T-shirt. "There are a lot of girls in this school and only *one* me. Think of all the hearts that are gonna get broken when I have to turn most of them down!"

Everyone groans.

Henry grins and takes another sugary bite.

"It's settled then," Sofia says, stepping to the head of the table. "We'll have games, food, and hayrides for families in the afternoon, and a Sadie Hawkins dance for middle school students that night. All in favor, say 'Aye.'"

"Aye!" everyone replies.

Annelise beams, pleased as punch that she got her way in the end. And why shouldn't she be happy? She is one of the prettiest and most popular girls in our school, even if she is bossy a lot of the time. She isn't shy around boys. It won't be any problem for her to ask someone to the dance. And whoever she asks will probably be too chicken to turn her down.

But I'm not like Annelise. I'm like *me* — Victoria Torres, unfortunately average. I've barely even asked a boy if I could borrow a pencil, much less asked him for a date! As the other kids start discussing the details of our Wild West event and divvying up responsibilities to make it happen, I fiddle with the donut on my napkin. Can I muster up enough courage to ask a boy to our school dance? And if I can, which boy should it be?

It would be easiest to ask someone like Henry or Sam, because we're good friends. Plus, it would be a lot of fun to hang out with either of them, helping with the food and games and then dancing around like crazy with all of our other friends that night.

But deep down, I want to ask the cutest and most popular boy in my class . . . my crush, Drew. If Drew were my date, I would shine brighter than the brightest star in the desert night sky.

I look across the table at my sister. I wish I could ask Sofia what I should do. But I can't tell her that I'm scared to ask a boy to the dance. Sofia is really good at taking charge and getting things done. She would just shake her head and tell me to stop acting so silly. Sofia even has a boyfriend this year. His name is Joey Thimble, and he lives down the street from us.

It's not like they're actually dating. Mom and Dad won't allow Sofia to go on real dates until she's older. They just walk to school together and stare at each other in the hallway between classes and study together on the weekends. It will be easy for Sofia to ask Joey to the dance because she already knows that he likes her.

But I have no idea if Drew likes me. I mean, we're friends, of course, so I know he *likes* me. But does he *like-like* me? If I ask him to go to the dance with me, will he say "Yes!", or will he say, "Sorry, Vicka, but I'm waiting for someone else to ask me"? That would be the most unfortunately embarrassing moment of my life!

Then again, what if he *did* say yes, and we went to the dance together? My hands would probably shake so much I'd spill cactus juice all over him. And dancing? I can barely walk down the hallway at school without tripping over my own feet. I'd be the one stepping on Drew's toes this time!

"Earth to Vicka," Henry says, giving me a nudge. "Do you want to help serve food in the chuck wagon, or don't you?" He taps the sign-up sheet that has appeared in front of me.

"Oh!" I say, coming out of my Drew daze. "Sure, I'll help!" Quickly, I brush the powdered sugar off my fingers and sign my name to the food booth sign-up sheet.

"Before everyone takes off, let's talk about what to do with the money we raise," Sofia says. "Principal Oates approved our plan to buy new laptops for the school library, but she suggested we do something for the community too, since we're asking the whole town to support our fund-raiser. Last year, the committee used part of the money they raised to build a new ramp for the skate park in town."

"That ramp is sweet!" Alex says. "I take a dive off it almost every weekend!"

"Me too!" Henry adds. "Hey, how about we donate another ramp to the skate park?"

"I think it would be better if we picked a different way to help the community this year," Sofia says. "That way we are reaching out to more people, not just the skaters. Any other suggestions?"

"We could ask people to swap a can of tuna or a box of cereal for carnival tickets," Will puts in. "My church group did that once for a fund-raiser. All the food we collected went to the local food pantry."

"That's a great idea," Laksha says. "My parents volunteer at the pantry. They always need more supplies. We could even set up a donation box now, by the office, and get kids to pitch in before the fund-raiser."

I perk up with a thought. "If we fill a donation box with food *before* the fund-raiser, and another one *during* it, does that mean Principal Oates will have to kiss a cow . . . twice?"

Everyone laughs and gives me high fives. They like the way I think! I'm back in the saddle.

"Okay, so it's agreed then?" Sofia says. "The money we raise at our Wild West fund-raiser will go toward new laptops for the library, plus we'll collect donations for the Middleton Food Pantry?"

"Aye!" everyone shouts.

"Yee-haw!" Henry adds. "We've got a plan!"

At supper later that night, Sofia and I tell Mom and Dad about our plans for the fund-raiser.

"I think a Wild West theme will be very popular!" Mom says. "There's something for everyone . . . good food, carnival games, hayrides for families, and a dance for the older kids that night."

"If you like, your mom and I could help chaperone the dance," Dad offers, looking at Mom. "We could even teach everyone a dance! Like the ol' Hat Dance!"

Sofia gasps. "*Please* tell me you're joking! I would die of embarrassment if you and Mom started dancing in front of my whole school!"

Dad grins. "We could even dig up a couple of sombreros to wear."

Sofia cringes.

"What's a *cat* dance?" Lucas asks, looking up from the mashed potato castle he's building on his dinner plate. Lucas is always turning his food into something else before he eats it. I think he will either grow up to be a famous cook or a great magician!

"The *Hat* Dance is the national dance of Mexico," Mom tells Lucas. "Here, let me show you."

Mom gets up from the table and takes Lucas by the hand. They stand, facing each other. "During a performance, the dancers place sombreros on the floor and dance around them while music plays. First, the dancers make a cup with their left hand and rest their right elbow in it," Mom explains, crooking her left arm across her middle and holding her right elbow in her left hand. Lucas copies her. "Good job, Lucas! Now switch, and hold your left elbow in your right hand."

Lucas follows along, catching on quickly, changing hand positions, back and forth between his left and right elbows.

"*Bueno!*" Mom says, encouraging him. "Now, keep doing that while hopping from one foot to the other, in time with the music. When the music changes, we link elbows and skip around in a circle."

"What music?" Lucas asks, looking around. Our dog, Poco, starts barking and frisking around Lucas's feet, but it doesn't sound like music to me!

"*This* music!" Dad says, dashing over to our piano. Soon Dad is playing a jazzy version of the Hat Dance tune. Abuela taught Sofia and me how to do the dance when we were Lucas's age. Sometimes she still gets us to do the dance with her at family picnics. Instead of sombreros, we just use baseball caps and beach hats!

As the dance comes to an end, Mom and Lucas do high fives while I give them a round of applause. Even Sofia claps along, laughing at Poco as he prances on his little legs, like he's eating up the spotlight!

As Mom, Dad, and Lucas sit down again, Sofia's eyes brighten with an idea. I can practically hear the gears turning in her head. "Live music *would* be kind of cool to have at our fund-raiser. Dad, could The Jalapeños play for our Sadie Hawkins dance? Not the whole time, but as a grand finale? Now that I think of it, everyone had a blast doing the Bunny Hop together at the Sock Hop last year. And on Valentine's Day, Principal Oates taught a bunch of us how to do the Cupid Shuffle in the Caf during lunch. It was hilarious! Maybe everyone would like learning the Hat Dance too, then we could jam to your band's music for a while!"

"What about me?" Lucas says. "I like jam! And I'm good at the Hat Dance too!"

Dad smiles, ruffling Lucas's hair. "Our whole family will help. And I'm sure The Jalapeños would love to play a gig at your school. I'll ask them when we rehearse this weekend."

Poco yips and chases around, like he wants to go to my school dance too! Even my dog is excited for the Sadie Hawkins. I wonder if I'll be the only member of my family who is too chicken to be there.

Before I go to bed later, I call Bea. I've been so busy with fund-raising stuff, I haven't had a chance to talk with her much today.

"The whole committee agreed to Annelise's plan," I tell her. "So our dance will for sure be a Sadie Hawkins. You know what that means? I have to ask a boy for a date! Every time I think about it, I shiver with goose bumps. Before long, I'll be sprouting chicken feathers! Bea, what should I do?"

"What should *you* do?" Bea replies. "What about me? I'm nervous about asking a boy to the dance too."

"But, Bea, you always know what I should do. When I wanted to be a cheerleader, you tried out with me. When we had class elections, you helped me run for president."

"Yes, but those were easy choices," Bea replies. "Now you're asking me to tell you what to do about a boy. Boys are a mystery to me this year. It was so much easier in grade school when all they did was chase us around the playground with worms and spiders. All we had to do was tell the teacher or gang up on them and chase them away."

I sigh. "Life was a lot less complicated then. Now that we're in middle school, everything is harder to understand . . . math . . . science . . . boys." I roll over onto my stomach and ask Bea a bigger question: "Who do you want to be your date? Henry?"

Bea doesn't answer right away. I bet her cheeks are blushing. She's had a secret crush on Henry all year long.

"I was thinking about it," she finally replies shyly. Even though Henry is the biggest goofball in our class, and Bea is a serious student, I think Henry is crushing on her too.

"What about you, Chicken Little?" Bea asks. "Do you want to ask Drew to the dance?"

I bite my lip. "I want to, but what if he says no?"

"He won't," Bea replies matter-of-factly. "Not if you ask him before someone else does."

"But how can you be *sure* he won't turn me down?" I ask.

"Because he likes you," Bea says.

"You don't know that!" I cry.

"Sure I do," Bea replies. "He gave you flowers, didn't he?"

I clam up. Someone *did* leave a flower for me in the band room after our holiday concert earlier this year. It might have been Drew, but the note wasn't signed, so I don't know for sure that it was from him. Even if he did leave the flower, it doesn't mean he *like*-likes me.

"But Drew gave flowers to you too, for helping him with his ensemble part," I say. "He's nice to everyone, not just me."

"I could ask him for you," Bea offers.

"No!" I exclaim. "Drew wouldn't want to go to the dance with a chicken!"

"But you said it yourself," Bea says. "You *are* chicken."

I grimace. "I know, but I don't want Drew to know that. I have to ask him myself or not at all."

Bea is quiet again, thinking. "Henry and Drew almost always go to the skate park on Saturday mornings. I see them there on my way to piano lessons. Tomorrow is Saturday. We could meet at the park after my lessons, find Drew and Henry, and ask them to the dance . . . together."

I gulp, nervously. "Um . . . but . . . I promised Abuela I'd help her plant flowers this weekend."

"We'll both help her," Bea says, her voice gaining confidence. "Right after we ask the boys for dates."

I gulp again and scratch my neck. I feel itchy all over. By tonight, I'll be covered in feathers. By tomorrow morning, I'll be craving chicken feed for breakfast. At least having Bea by my side will make the whole situation a little less scary. Besides, Drew and Henry are best friends too. Do boys get scared, the same as girls? If they do, maybe it will be less scary for them to say yes if they get to say it together.

"Okay, we'll ask them at the skate park tomorrow," I tell Bea, with as much confidence as I can muster. Half of me is excited to ask the boys to the dance, but the other half of me might just flap my wings and fly away!

Chapter 5

Jazmin to the Rescue

The next morning, Bea texts me after her piano lesson.

> On my way to the park. Meet me there. K?

My palms are sweaty and my thumb shakes as I type a reply.

>  K

Ten minutes later, I'm biking up the steep hill that leads to the skate park. Actually, I'm walking up it, pushing my bike. It's easier to push it than to huff and puff as I pedal my legs off, trying to bike up it. When

I get to the top of the hill, I hop on my bike again and cruise down the other side. I can see the skate park now. A bunch of kids are there, practicing tricks on the ramps and rails, but I'm zooming so fast, I can't tell if any of them are Drew or Henry.

As I put on the brakes at the bottom of the hill, I see Bea pedaling up the path from the other direction. We meet in the middle, right outside the entrance to the skate park.

"Ready?" Bea asks, climbing off her bike and hanging her backpack of piano music on the handlebars.

"For anything," I say, even though I'm shaking in my sneakers. "But I don't see Drew and Henry any-where. Maybe they didn't come to the park to —"

"Hey, Vicka! Hi, Bea!" someone calls out.

We turn around and see Drew and Henry waving. A moment later, they hop on their boards and skate toward us. I grip the handlebars on my bike tighter as I park it next to Bea's. I was hoping Bea and I could go over our plan one more time. After I agreed to ask Drew, we discussed everything in detail on the phone last night. It was easy then, but now that I'm face-to-face with my crush, I can't even remember what we decided to say!

"What are you two doing here?" Henry asks, skidding to a stop in front of us. He's wearing a pair of shades that say *#1 Skater* on the sides. Every month, kids from our school organize a skateboard demonstration here. They come up with goofy prizes to give away for best trick and most improved. The kid who is named best skater at the demo gets to wear the *#1 Skater* sunglasses until the next competition. Henry must have won last month.

Henry smiles at Bea. "I didn't know you liked skateboarding!"

"We don't," Bea replies. "I mean, we *do*, but that's not why we're here."

"Are you looking for Jenny?" Drew asks. "She isn't here yet."

Our friend, Jenny, loves to skateboard. She's into lots of different kinds of sports. She's even trying to get Bea and me to join her summer softball team. We're thinking about it.

I shake my head. "No, not Jenny," I reply.

"Who then?" Henry asks.

"You," Bea blurts out. Then she bites her lip nervously and ducks her eyes.

Henry puffs up his chest. "Join the club," he jokes. "*Everyone* is looking for me!" Drew shakes his head, snickering. Bea blushes three shades of pink.

At least Henry's funny reply makes me relax a little. I glance at Bea, but she's still studying her shoelaces. I'm going to have to take the lead.

"Um," I say, pushing up my glasses, "it's just that . . . I was wondering . . . that is, *we* were wondering . . . if you guys would like to . . . I mean, it's fine if you *don't* want to, but if you *do* want to . . . then maybe we could, um . . ."

"Spit it out, Vicka," Henry says impatiently. "Moss is starting to grow on my skateboard."

Drew gives Henry the elbow. "Give her a chance, Hen," he says.

"Right," Henry replies. "Sorry, Vicka. What were you saying?"

But before I can take another crack at my question, I hear a familiar voice call out from down the bike path. "Yoo-hoo . . . *Dre-ewww!*" Annelise waves as she bikes up the path, a pack of girls pedaling behind her, including Katie, Grace, and Julia.

"Hi, guys!" all the girls singsong as they park their bikes and walk up to us.

"We came to watch you skateboard," Annelise says, stepping in front of Bea and me. "Especially you, Drew." She barks a laugh. "'You Drew' . . . that rhymes! I'm a poet and didn't know *it!*"

All the girls giggle and huddle up around the boys, launching into a conversation about skate-boarding. Annelise even gets Drew to teach her a trick. Everyone bursts out laughing when she lands flat on her butt. They stop quickly when Annelise gives them a warning glare.

As other girls try the trick too, Bea and I slink away, pushing our bikes down the path toward Abuela's house to help her plant flowers. No way can we ask Henry and Drew to the dance today.

"Well, that was pathetic," Bea says, glancing back when we get out of earshot. "I turned into a stone statue when I tried to ask Henry for a date to the dance."

"At least you didn't turn into a babbling brook," I reply. "I'm surprised fish didn't leap out of my mouth while I tried to ask Drew."

My comment makes Bea giggle. "When did Annelise and her friends learn how to talk to boys without clamming up or rambling?"

I shrug. "We must have been absent from school that day."

As we climb on our bikes and start pedaling up the hill, Bea says, "We need help."

"Lots of help," I add, standing up to make the pedaling a little easier. "But who do we ask? Abuela is always willing to help me, but this doesn't feel like a grandmother problem."

Bea pedals harder, thinking. "There's only one person who can teach us how to talk to boys."

"Who?" I ask, stopping halfway up the steep hill. My legs feel like jelly. I start walking my bike the rest of the way.

"My sister," Bea replies, climbing off her bike and walking it too.

"Jazmin?" I say. Bea's sister is an eighth grader, just like Sofia.

Bea nods. "She's always helping her friends with their boy problems. Let's stop at my house first and talk to her."

When we get to the top of the hill, we hop on our bikes again and zoom down the other side. Jazmin is one of the most popular girls at our school. She's even a cheerleader! If anyone can teach us how to be braver around boys, it's her.

"Do you think Jazmin will help us?" I ask as we hop off our bikes at Bea's house a few minutes later.

Bea gives me a tentative nod. "She will if she's in a good mood. It's hard to tell with Jaz, sometimes. She can be sweet and smiley one minute and then, for no reason, sock you with a pillow the next."

"Sofia is like that too. I think she has a mood switch inside her. One minute it's *off*, and the next it's turned all the way *on*."

Bea takes a deep breath and links arms with me. "There's only one way to find out if Jazmin's mood switch is on or off today," she says. "Let's go find her."

Bea and I head inside her house and upstairs to Jazmin's room.

Softly, we knock on her door.

No answer.

I look at Bea.

Bea bites her lip. "She's probably listening to music. We'll have to knock harder."

"Whatever you say . . ."

We knock again. *Harder.*

Still no answer.

"Are you sure she's in there?" I ask, pressing my ear against the door. Silence.

"Positive," Bea says. "Every Saturday she sleeps until lunchtime, then grabs a bowl of cereal and goes back to her room until supper."

"Maybe she's still sleeping," I whisper.

"She can't be," Bea whispers back. "Jazmin snores like a chainsaw. She must have her earbuds in. We'll have to knock the door off its hinges before she hears us."

"Let's try texting her," I suggest. "No matter what Sofia is doing, she always hears her phone when a message drops in."

Bea's eyes brighten. "Brilliant idea, Vicka!" she tells me. I smile. Best friends can make you shine in an instant!

Bea takes out her phone and types a text to her sister.

> Open ur door.
> B & V

Bea sends the message. A moment later, we hear a phone chime in Jazmin's room. A moment after that, the door swings open. There stands Bea's sister, her hair bunched up in a messy topknot. She's wearing dark rimmed glasses instead of contacts, baggy pajamas, and fuzzy slippers. She looks as average as me on a normal Saturday morning.

"Yeah?" Jazmin says, plucking out her earbuds and sticking her phone into the pocket on her pajama top.

"We need advice," Bea tells her sister.

I nod. "*Expert* advice. That's why we came to you."

My *expert* comment makes Jazmin smile. I was hoping it might. Abuela once told me paying compliments to others doesn't cost a thing, but doing so can make you rich with friends.

"What seems to be the problem?" Jazmin asks me.

Quickly, I come to the point of our visit. "The problem is . . . boys," I say.

Bea nods. "We want to ask two boys from our class for dates to the Sadie Hawkins dance, but we don't know how."

Jazmin nods knowingly. "I guess I can give you a tip or two." She steps aside and motions us into her room.

The only other times I've been in Jazmin's bedroom were when Bea and I snuck in, looking for outfits to "borrow" or her diary to snoop through. I never took time to really look around because we were scared silly that we would get caught. Now I can see the cool posters she has hanging on her walls, bed pillows that are as fuzzy as her slippers, sketches of goth fairies and villains tacked above her desk. I inhale deeply. Her room smells like a sweet mix of honeysuckle and ginger. I make a mental note to start smelling better, ASAP.

"Have a seat," Jazmin tells us, motioning to her bed. Bea and I sit down as Jazmin pulls up a chair. She crosses her legs casually, swinging her slippered foot and twisting a strand of loose hair around her finger. "Boys really aren't that complicated," she tells us. "If you want them to say yes to you, the first thing you have to do is get their attention. The best way to do that is to offer them something irresistible. Food is best. Seriously, middle school boys are part caveman."

"Food?" Bea says. "Like snacky stuff?"

Jazmin nods. "The snackier the better."

I scoot back on the bed and crisscross my legs. Jazmin is right. If there's one thing every boy in my class loves, it's food! Especially if it's sweet.

"But you can't just hand a boy a plate of cookies, or he'll scarf them down and be on his way." Jazmin laughs. "Boys have the attention span of houseflies. You've got to catch them off guard, hold their attention, then pop the question before they buzz off."

"But how do we do that?" I ask. "How do we catch them off guard and ask them to the dance?"

"You could try making up a poem or jingle," Jazmin replies. "Like 'It would be *sweet* to go to the dance with you!' Attach it to a bag of chocolate kisses. Or write, 'Will you *stick* with me at Sadie Hawkins?' and leave it with a package of gum on his desk."

Bea and I bounce excitedly. "Those are good ideas!" Bea says. "Thanks, Jaz!"

Jazmin smiles. "My pleasure, sis. By the way, which boys are you two going to ask?"

Bea and I exchange glances. Saying Drew's name out loud feels like it might jinx me. Bea must feel the same way because she doesn't mention Henry's name, either.

"Um . . . we're still working on that," I finally say.

"I'm sure any boy would be happy to go with either of you," Jazmin says. "You could ask them together. You know, a double date? Especially if the two guys are friends."

"We tried that this morning at the skate park," I confess. "But a bunch of other girls got in our way."

"Don't give up," Jazmin says. "Find a time when there aren't so many people around, and try again. But don't wait too long. If you do, some other girls are sure to ask them before you get a chance!"

As Bea and I head down to the kitchen in search of a snack before we bike to Abuela's — hey, girls like sweet stuff too! — we make a pledge to each other. Today, we put together a plan. Then, first thing Monday morning, we ask Drew and Henry to the dance!

Chapter 6

A Drew Dilemma

I can barely eat breakfast on Monday morning, thinking about asking Drew to the dance today.

Bea and I bought giant candy bars at the dollar store this weekend and designed super cute notes with my mom's scrapbooking supplies. She even had these cute little candy stickers!

Then we signed our names and attached the notes to the candy bars.

IT WOULD BE SWEET TO GO TO SADIE HAWKINS WITH YOU!

All we have to do is find Drew and Henry, hand them the candy, and wait for them to read the notes. Then all our problems will be solved, and we'll have dates to the dance!

That's what I keep telling myself, at least. But the truth is, I've barely eaten or slept since we made the notes. Last night I even dreamed that my candy bar turned into a skateboard the moment I gave it to Drew. He read the note, shrieked in terror, then hopped on the board and zoomed away!

¡Uf! Something tells me our sweet plan might go sour.

Still, I can't chicken out. I promised Bea to go through with it today, so I grab my backpack, tuck the candy bar and note inside, and head out the door.

My heart is beating faster than the Mexican Hat Dance all the way to school. As soon as I get to our sixth-grade wing, Annelise runs up to me. "Did you get my text?" she asks.

"No," I say, patting my pockets, looking for my phone. I must have left it at home in my hurry to get to school before chickening out.

"We're having a special fund-raiser meeting before the first bell," she tells me. "Ditch your stuff and get down to the library, fast."

I frown. "What do you mean? Sofia didn't say anything to me about a special meeting this morning."

"That's because I just called it," Annelise says smugly.

"You can't do that!" I say. "Sofia is in charge of the committee. Besides, I've got important things to do before the bell rings!" I look up and down the hall. No sign of Bea yet — or Drew and Henry.

Annelise makes a face. "What could be more important than coming to *my* meeting?"

I cringe. I can't tell Annelise that Bea and I are going to ask the boys to the dance this morning. She'll probably come snooping around and ruin the whole thing.

"Never mind," I grumble. "I'll be there."

Annelise smiles and snags a thick packet from her locker. I see the logo for her dad's ad agency printed on the front of it before she takes off down the hall to the library.

We aren't supposed to have a committee meeting until later in the week. And Sofia will *not* be happy that Annelise didn't check with her first. But Annelise has a mind of her own. If she wants something done, she does it, no questions asked.

I toss my backpack into my locker and head down the hall. Honestly? I'm a tiny bit relieved there has been a change of plans. If the meeting goes long, I won't have time to give Drew my candy bar and note before first hour. I hate to break a promise to Bea, but I can't shake my fear of following through with it either.

"What's the big emergency?" Henry asks when we all gather in the library a few minutes later.

"It's not an emergency," Annelise replies. "I have good news! I knew everyone would want to hear it right away."

Sofia frowns from her seat at the head of the table. "In the future, Annelise, please check with me before you call a special meeting. I'm in charge here," she says.

Annelise brushes aside Sofia's comment like a pile of cookie crumbs. "My news is too important to save until our next meeting," she says, opening the packet in front of her and pulling out a stack of posters. "My dad made these over the weekend! Aren't they the coolest thing ever?!"

She holds up one of the big, glossy posters. It looks like an old-fashioned WANTED poster. The kind you see nailed to a post in a cowboy movie.

"That's not all," Annelise continues. "He put in an order for cowboy hats and dance tickets too!

We should have them by the end of the week. Of course, he's donating everything."

Everyone is super excited about the posters and cowboy hats. Even Sofia sets aside her grumpiness to thank Annelise. "Please thank your dad for us too," she adds. "The posters look awesome. Everyone will want to buy cowboy hats and wear them to the fund-raiser!"

"Of course they will," Annelise replies. "That's why I thought of it."

"I talked to my grandparents about giving people hayrides," Alex puts in. "They said okay! They'll bring a cow to the dance too, so Principal Oates can give it a kiss if we collect a ton of food for the pantry."

"That's great, Alex!" Sofia says.

"Yeah, Alex, please thank your grandparents for us," Annelise adds.

Sofia scowls.

"Do you think they could bring a few extra hay bales for decorating the gym?" Will asks. "I was thinking we could paint a backdrop for a photo booth. A big red barn, maybe. I'm pretty handy with a paint-brush. Anyway, if we set hay bales in front of the backdrop, couples could sit on them while they get their picture taken during the dance."

"That's an awesome idea, Will!" Laksha exclaims. "Who can we get to take the pictures?"

"I'll borrow the school's camera and take the pho-tos myself," Sofia says. "I do that a lot for the school's website."

"I can help you paint the backdrop, Will," Annelise says. "I'm an excellent artist."

"Um . . . sure," Will says, his ears pinking up. "I'll talk to Mr. Tate about using the art room to work on it."

Annelise smiles.

Other kids offer to hunt around at home for more stuff to decorate the gym — checkered table cloths, camp lanterns, mason jars, washtubs, quilts, horseshoes . . . anything to turn our gym into a cool barnyard scene. As we all take some of the posters to hang up around school and in town, Sofia has us sign up to sell dance tickets and cowboy hats in the Caf next week.

Everything is really starting to come together! But the thought of getting my picture taken with my date at the dance makes my stomach swirl. What if I don't get a date at all? Will I have to get my picture taken sitting solo on a hay bale?

The bell rings for first hour. We all hurry off to class. No time to ask Drew for a date now. I breathe a sigh of relief.

By lunchtime, posters are up all over the school and everyone is buzzing about the dance. Some girls have already gotten their dates! Our friend Jenny has even asked Sam to the dance. "We're just going as friends," she tells Bea and me. "We'll help out with the games at the carnival, then go to the dance that night."

I'm super excited for Jenny. She and Sam get along great, so I know they'll have a blast. I'm friends with Drew too, but having a crush on him complicates things. It's weird, but when you like a boy just as a friend, it's easy to be around him. Unfortunately, when you *like-like* him, you can barely even look at him! I know that doesn't make sense, but it's true.

"So have you two asked anyone to the dance yet?" Jenny asks Bea and me as we head to the Caf for lunch.

Annelise pokes into our conversation as we walk past her. "Well?" she says, falling into step with us. "Have you?"

"Not me," Bea says.

"Me either," I chime in. "How about you, Annelise?"

Annelise pulls us off to the side, like she was just waiting for us to ask. "No, but I've got it all planned out," she replies. "When *my* date gets his invitation, there's no way he will turn it down!"

"Why? Are you going to shove him inside a locker until he agrees?" Jenny asks.

Bea and I snicker.

Annelise makes a face. "Very funny," she says to Jenny.

"What then?" I ask.

Annelise's eyes sparkle with mischief. "I don't want to give away my secret yet," she replies. "But I'm letting all the girls know my guy is off limits until the skateboard demo in two weeks! My dad can't get a pickup truck until then."

Bea, Jenny, and I gape at Annelise. "You can't hog one of the guys for yourself!" I tell her.

"Why not?" Annelise replies. "The whole dance was *my* idea, remember?"

I clamp my mouth shut.

"Who's the *lucky* guy?" Jenny asks sarcastically.

Annelise flicks back her hair and looks at us like the answer is obvious. "The most popular boy in our class, of course."

I stiffen.

Bea gasps.

Jenny glances at me.

"Spread the word for me, girls," Annelise says, lifting her chin. "*Drew* will be going to the dance with *me!*"

As Annelise flutters away, I freeze into a solid block of ice. "If I ask Drew to the dance before Annelise does, she will *murder* me!" I tell my friends. "But if I don't ask Drew before the skateboard demo, he will probably say yes to Annelise, since no one else has asked him to go. Then I'll have to watch Annelise dancing with my crush while I cook hot dogs in the chuck wagon! Drew will never know that I wanted to ask him in the first place."

Bea gives my arm a firm squeeze. "Annelise doesn't get to tell us who we can or can't ask to the dance."

Jenny nods in agreement. "She doesn't rule the school. If you want Drew to be your date, you've got to ask him. *Now.* Before Annelise puts her big plan into action." Jenny shakes her head. "What was that about a pickup truck? Is she planning to lasso Drew and haul him to the dance? It will serve her right not to get her way for a change."

I cringe. Even though I agree with my friends, being right doesn't make my choice any easier.

Chapter 7

Musical Smiles

All week, girls are coming up with clever ways to ask boys to the Sadie Hawkins dance. One girl brought a bouquet of helium balloons to school and tied them to her date's locker with a note that said, "I will be *flying high* if you go to Sadie Hawkins with me!"

Other girls used sidewalk chalk to write notes outside the entrance to our school. When their dates arrived, they saw their names printed in big block letters on the sidewalk, asking them to the dance. Katie, Grace, and Julia even bought old LP records from my family's music store and sang to their dates in front

of the whole Caf! Then they gave them notes, written on the albums.

But ever since Annelise announced her plan to ask Drew to the dance, I've been dragging my feet. Bea is trying to be patient with me, but I can tell she's getting really antsy to ask Henry. At first, she was chicken to ask him, but now she's afraid someone else will beat her to it if she doesn't ask him soon.

I've been stalling for time, making up excuses because I'm afraid to ask Drew before Annelise does. But I'm also afraid of missing my chance to go to the dance with him. I've been accidentally-on-purpose forgetting to bring my candy bar and note to school every day this week. Today, I "forgot" to bring it again.

"No worries," Bea says when I tell her my lame excuse. "I bought an extra candy bar last night and wrote a new note for you." She pulls two bars of chocolate from her backpack and shows me the one with a note addressed to Drew. "All you have to do is sign your name!"

"Er . . . thanks," I say.

Bea gives me a big smile. "That's what friends are for."

"But . . . I . . . uh . . ." I search my unfortunately average brain for a new excuse as Bea puts the extra candy bar and note into my hand. But I am fresh out of excuses. If I don't ask Drew today, Bea will give up on me ever asking him. Maybe she'll even give up on being my friend!

"It's Friday," Bea continues, "so we'll see the boys at band practice this afternoon. Let's get to the band room early. I'll sneak my candy bar into Henry's tuba case. You can leave your candy bar on the kettle drums. Drew will find it as soon as he gets to the percussion section. We'll have their answers before we even play a note!"

I give Bea a weak smile. Her plan is excellent, but my confidence is wimping out.

"I . . . I . . . I have a better idea," I say, thinking fast. "Let's wait until Monday to ask them! We have band practice then too. We can . . . um . . . bake cookies over the weekend! We'll make them in the shape of musical notes. Get it? Musical cookies in the band room? The guys will love that!"

I give Bea my best, most hopeful smile.

Unfortunately, Bea frowns. She takes the candy bar from me and puts it in our locker, then closes the door. *Clunk!*

"No more excuses, Vicka," she says. Her tone is kind but firm. "We are asking the boys at band practice. *Today.*"

I feel as jittery as a jumping bean all afternoon. Even though I would fight off poisonous snakes and giant girl-eating spiders for my best friend, I wait out of sight until I see Bea take her candy bar from our locker before band practice.

When she's gone, I lag behind in the hallway until the bell rings. Then, instead of dashing off to the band room to meet up with Bea, I open our locker and start tossing out old gum wrappers and quiz sheets that are crumpled on the bottom shelf. Then I tidy up our door magnets and alphabetize all our text-books. But as I start to rearrange our class folders from lightest to darkest, the candy bar I'm supposed to be leaving for Drew at this very moment falls to my feet.

Thunk!

I pick it up and think about Bea. She must have put her note in Henry's tuba case by now. Soon, she will have her answer. As for me, my answer will stay stuck in the middle — somewhere between yes and no.

All Bea wanted was for us to go to the dance together, I think. *Now I've broken my promise to her again. I'm the* worst *best friend in the world.*

Unwrapping the candy bar, I take a bite. I keep biting and swallowing, barely tasting the sweet chocolate as I gulp it down. When the candy is gone, I throw away the wrapper and trudge off to the band room.

"Where were you?!" Bea asks, looking up from her seat in the flute section. Everyone is already here, warming up their instruments.

I slip in next to her and open my flute case. "Um . . . I was running late. Sorry."

"Did you leave your candy bar and note for Drew?" She glances back toward the percussion section. I glance too. Drew is standing by the kettle drums, talking with some of the other percussionists.

"Um . . . I . . . well . . . the thing is . . ." I mutter. "I couldn't find it! I mean, I think someone ate it."

Bea makes a face. "But I left it in our locker! No one could eat it." Then she gives me a very serious squint. "Is that *chocolate* on your chin?"

My hand flies to my face, just as a deep note bellows from the brass section. Bea and I turn around to see Henry waving at us over his tuba. He plays a fanfare on his tuba, then holds up the candy bar Bea left for him and gives her a big smile.

Bea gasps, facing forward again, her cheeks blushing bright pink. "I think that means he'll go to the dance with me!" she says, beaming.

I rub chocolate from my chin, gulping down my guilt. "I'm so sorry I didn't keep my promise to ask Drew today. I know that was an awful thing to do, but I'm still afraid of what Annelise will do if I ask him. Plus, what if he says *no* to my invitation? What if he says *yes?* Please don't be mad at me."

But Bea is flying too high on Henry's answer to be mad at anyone. "Of course I'm not mad at you! Just bring a new candy bar to school next week . . ." She glances back and gives Henry a shy wave as our band director, Mr. Ono, steps onto his podium. Henry grins, then takes a bite from the candy bar.

Bea leans toward me again and adds in a low voice, "You've got to do it before the skateboard demo, Vicka. I overheard Annelise talking to Grace in the instrument room before band. She's going to dress up in a cowgirl outfit and arrive at the skate park in a fancy pickup truck! After cheering for Drew at the demo, she's going to whisk him off to the Lazy L Riding Stables. While they're riding their horses out on the trail, she'll ask him to the dance. When Grace asked her why she doesn't just do it school, Annelise goes, 'Because bigger is better.'" Bea rolls her eyes. "Her dad is paying for the whole thing, of course."

I shake my head. "Isn't that a bit over the top? It's not a marriage proposal!"

Bea shrugs. "Anything for Annelise."

As Mr. Ono lifts his baton, Bea gives me one last desperate look. "There's no way Drew can turn down an invitation like that, Vicka. You've *got* to ask him before Annelise does!"

I grip my flute, counting measures until it's our turn to join the song. Bea and I went to the riding stables for Katie's birthday party last fall. It was super fun. We got to ride our horses down wooded trails, gallop across an open field, and pick apples in an orchard. Afterward we rode our horses back to the stables and brushed them down. We each got a Lazy L lanyard to wear for keeps. Annelise and Drew are sure to have a good time at the stables too.

If I ask Drew to the dance and he says yes, Annelise will have a fit! Her dad will probably be angry at me too, since he's paying for her big plan. What if he gets so mad he refuses to help with the fund-raiser?

We're supposed to start selling cowboy hats and dance tickets on Monday. If Annelise's dad changes his mind, the whole committee will be upset with me, including Sofia. All her plans to host the best fund-raiser in the history of our school will evaporate like a science experiment. And it will all be because of *me*.

I glance back at the percussion section while Mr. Ono works with the trumpets on a tricky part in our song. Drew is standing by the bass drum now, waiting for his turn to play.

He catches my eye, grins at me, then pretends to conk himself over the head with the big, soft drum mallet in his hand. He crosses his eyes and wags his head like there are cartoon stars circling around him. When he sees me giggling, he smiles again. Not a goofy, cartoon smile. It's an *I-like-you* smile.

I turn away so quickly I knock my flute against my music stand. *Clunk!*

Mr. Ono looks over from his podium. "Be careful, Vicka!" he says. "Flutes dent easily."

I sink down in my chair. *¡Uf!* Fortunately, Drew

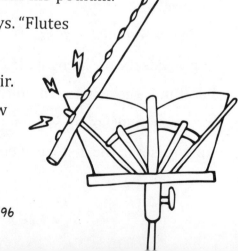

can't see my cheeks turning pink. I'm blushing with embarrassment for bashing my flute, but mostly I'm blushing because of Drew's smile.

First chance I get, I will ask him, I think, lifting my flute to my mouth. *I will* not *chicken out this time . . . not . . . not . . . not . . . probably not.*

Chapter 8

Sweets for the Sweet

Running upstairs to my bedroom after school, I stand in front of the mirror that hangs behind my door. My dad is always telling us "practice makes perfect." Usually, he's talking about practicing an instrument, like my flute, because he's totally into making good music. But practice is good for other things too. Maybe if I practice talking to Drew before I ask him to the dance, I won't chicken out again.

While walking home, I stopped at the dollar store to buy another candy bar. I decided that the Caf would be the best place to ask Drew to the dance. We have lunch at the same time, so I always see him there. If I watch for him to come in, we can meet up at the milk cooler. Then I'll plunk the candy bar down on his tray. That will catch him off guard, just like Jazmin suggested.

When he looks up in surprise, I'll ask him to the dance. No note this time. Just me, Victoria Torres, unfortunately terrified.

Poco is watching from my bed, but I don't mind. He won't tell anyone that I'm practicing asking a boy on a date. And somehow, it makes me feel more confident having him here. He may be a dog, but he's a member of our family. Like Sofia said, families have to stick together. It helps knowing Poco is here, sticking with me.

I pick up the candy bar I bought for Drew. Then I square my shoulders in front of my mirror, close my eyes, and imagine Drew standing by the milk cooler in the Caf at school, sifting through the mini-cartons, looking for a chocolate milk. I walk confidently up to him and pretend to set the candy bar on his tray.

When Drew looks at me, I open my eyes and pretend my reflection is him.

"Hi, Drew! Happy National Candy Bar Day!" I say cheerfully into the mirror. It sounds hokey, even now, but it's the best opening line I could come up with. Like Jazmin said, boys have the attention span of a housefly. And I have the confidence of an ant. I have to get his attention quickly, or I'll never ask him at all.

From the corner of my mouth I say in a deeper voice, "Hi, Vicka! Wow, I didn't know it was National Candy Bar Day today. I didn't even know it existed."

I laugh along with my Drew-reflection, then say, "Well, now you do! In celebration, we'll be selling candy bars at our Wild West fund-raiser next weekend. Are you going?"

My Drew-reflection nods. "I'll be at the carnival, but no one has asked me to the dance yet. I heard a rumor that Annelise is planning to ask me. I guess I'll have to go with her if no one else asks first."

Casually, I push my glasses up higher on the bridge of my nose and tuck a strand of hair behind my ear. "Well, Drew, if you'd like, we could go to the dance together."

Now my Drew-reflection perks up. His adorable eyebrows rise a notch higher on his cute forehead. His smile is warm enough to melt the chocolate. "That would totally rock, Vicka! Thanks! I'm in!"

I smile like the most confident girl in the world. "It's a date, Drew."

My Drew-reflection smiles gratefully.

I turn away from the mirror and march to my bed. Then I collapse onto it. Poco barks, then gives my cheek a congratulatory lick.

"Thanks, Poco." I set the candy bar aside and pull my pooch in for a hug. Pretending to shine is so much easier than shining in real life.

Just then, I hear giggling coming from the other side of my bedroom door. Poco looks over and cocks his head. *Woof?*

Quickly, I jump up and fling the door open. There stands my little brother, giggling into his hands.

"Lucas!" I shout. "Were you eavesdropping on me?!" Even though he's only five, I can't help but be embarrassed that someone heard me.

Lucas stops laughing and shakes his head. "No," he says. "I was just listening to you talk to yourself."

I punch my fists into my hips. "That *is* eavesdropping, Lucas. And it's not nice." I pull him into my room and close the door. "Now tell me exactly what you heard."

Lucas hops onto my bed, pulling Poco onto his lap. "First, you talked like you always do. Then you talked in a made-up voice, like Daddy does when he tells me that story about the Bear Prince."

"*El Príncipe Oso?*" I ask, sitting down next to him.

Lucas nods, petting Poco. "Daddy always makes his voice low and scratchy when Señor Oso talks in that story. It sounded like you did, just now." Lucas growls like the bear in the Mexican folktale our parents like to tell us. In the story, the bear is actually an enchanted prince.

Poco jumps to his tiny feet, barking at my bear-brother.

Lucas laughs, scooping up our dog again. "Don't worry, Poco, it's just me!" he says in his regular voice. "I'm not really a bear. Be good and maybe Vicka will let us play art class with her."

I make a puzzled face. "Art class?"

Lucas nods, excitedly. "I heard you say you *drew* something. What was it? A robot? I'm really good at drawing robots!"

"I wasn't talking about anything I *drew*," I reply. "I was having a pretend conversation with someone *named* Drew. He's a boy in my class."

"Oh," Lucas says. "Why were you pretending to talk to a boy? Can't you talk to him for real?"

"Yes, but I want to ask him to go to the school dance with me. Every time I try to ask him, I chicken out. I thought it might help to practice."

Lucas frowns. "Why are you scared to ask him to the dance? You ask me to do stuff all the time . . . help set the table . . . make waffles for breakfast . . . go to the park to play . . ."

"This is different, Lucas," I say. "You're my brother. It's easy to talk to you because we're family. Drew isn't family. He's just . . . a friend."

Lucas thinks this through. "Do you mean *boy*-friend? Sophie is always practice-talking to that neighbor boy she likes."

"Joey?" I say, surprised. "Sofia practices talking to him?" I can't help but feel a little better about my practice conversation, knowing that my perfect sister practices talking to boys too.

Lucas nods. "My room is right next to her room. I hear her talking all the time."

"Lucas," I start, shaking my head at my brother, "it isn't nice to listen in on other people's conversations, even if they're only talking to themselves. You shouldn't do it."

"Then you and Sofia should learn to talk quieter," he replies, hopping down from my bed. "Can I go now? My favorite show is starting soon, and Mommy said I can watch it."

I give Lucas a nod. He skips to my door. Poco follows after him.

Suddenly Lucas stops and hurries back to me. "I hope that Drew boy wants to go to the dance with you, Vicka," he says. "But if he doesn't, I'll be your date!"

I smile at my little brother. Then I give him a great big hug.

"Thanks, Lucas," I say, squeezing him tight. "That's the sweetest thing you've ever said to me."

Lucas wriggles out of my hug.

Without thinking twice, I pick up the candy bar I bought for Drew and give it to my little brother. "Sweets for the sweet," I tell him.

"Thanks, Vicka!" he shouts. He skips away with the candy bar, Poco yipping at his heels.

I smile as I watch them go. Sometimes a little brother can be a pain in the neck. But, sometimes, he can be your best friend too.

I look at my empty hands. No note and no candy bar for my crush. I really am down to the one and only me.

Chapter 9

Dance Hats

On Monday, Bea is still flying high, joking around with Henry, practicing their do-si-do steps down the hall, and making plans for the Western costumes they'll wear to the dance. I want to talk to her about my plan to ask Drew at lunch today, but I don't want to interrupt all their fun.

I wonder if Drew and I will goof around like that if he agrees to be my date for the dance. It would be fun if we could all dress up in costumes and goof around together. Quickly, I take out my phone and send Bea a text.

> Today. At lunch. I'll ask him. Wish me luck!

I smile when I see Bea's reply.

> Good luck!!!

When I get to the Caf later, I grab a taco, sit down, and barely eat it as I watch for Drew. Sam and Will are selling dance tickets and cowboy hats near the Caf doors. Lots of kids are waiting in line to buy them. I have to crane my neck to see past the crowd as I keep an eye out for Drew. As soon as he walks in, I'll hurry over to the milk cooler and ask him to the dance.

But Drew doesn't show. When Bea finally arrives, I take my food tray to the dish room counter and hurry over to her.

"Did you ask him yet?" Bea asks excitedly.

I shake my head and frowned. "He isn't here. Where could he be? He always eats lunch at the same time as me."

"Uh-oh," Bea says. "I just remembered something. Henry is eating lunch in the library today. So is Jenny. They're making plans for the skate demo on Saturday. I bet Drew is there too."

My shoulders sag. Jenny said something to me about the meeting in the hallway earlier, but I was so focused on my Drew problem, I barely heard her. "There goes my plan," I say. "I was going to ask him, then buy dance tickets and cowboy hats for both of us."

Bea gives me a confident smile. "You can still ask him. I know for a *fact* Drew will say yes to you."

I give Bea a suspicious squint. "How do you know that for a fact? Did you say something to him??"

She doesn't answer.

"Bea! You promised you wouldn't ask him for me!"

"I didn't ask him," Bea replies. "I only mentioned to Henry that it would be fun if all four of us could go to the dance together. You know, BFFs and BFFs? Henry thinks it's a great idea too."

I growl like a grumpy bear. "Great, Henry probably told Drew what you said. He must be wondering why it's taking me so long to ask him. He probably thinks I don't want to go to the dance with him at all!"

"Just *ask* him," Bea insists. "Do it by the lockers between classes. Or at Java Jane's after school. Or at lunch tomorrow! Then you'll know."

But when I see Drew by the lockers after lunch, he's surrounded by his skating buddies. And when I peek inside Java Jane's after school, he's sitting at a booth, laughing at something one of his friends is showing everyone on her screen. Tomorrow I have to sell dance tickets during lunch, so I can't ask him then.

Should I text him now? I have his phone number because we studied together for math club a few times, but that was weeks ago. I haven't texted him since. What if he shows the text to his friends, and they all laugh at the fact that Victoria Torres wants to go to the dance with him?

I cringe at the thought, then slip out of Java Jane's and hurry down the sidewalk before he sees me spying on him.

The next day, I stop by the office before lunch to pick up the dance tickets and cowboy hats we're selling for the fund-raiser. Laksha was supposed to help me today, but she's home sick so Bea offered to lend me a hand.

"Did you ask you-know-*who* to the dance yet?" Bea asks as we take hats from a big box and stack them in a tall tower on a table in the Caf.

I shake my head. "Nope. What's wrong with me, Bea? I must be the most unfortunately average chicken around."

"You're my favorite chicken," Bea says, putting on one of the hats. "And the *best* BFF around, whether or not you ask you-know-*Drew* to the dance." She gives me a smile.

I take a bunch of dance tickets from the cash box Principal Oates gave to me while Bea sets up a sign at the end of our table.

Howdy, Pard'ners!
Get Your Cowboy Hats
and
Sadie Hawkins Tickets Here!

A group of seventh-grade girls walk into the Caf and hurry over to our table. They buy six dance tickets and three hats, chatting about how much fun they will have with their dates.

"I'm going to buy an outfit at that Western shop in the mall this weekend," one of the girls says to the others. "Y'all should come along and buy outfits too!"

As they walk away making weekend plans, more kids come to the table. As Bea sells them tickets and hats, I slouch down and mutter, "While those girls are having fun shopping at the mall, Bea will be hanging out with Henry after the skateboard demo, and Annelise will be horseback riding with Drew at the *Lazy L* stables. Me? I'll be sitting at home, watching goofy cartoons with my little brother!"

"I like watching goofy cartoons," a voice says.

Looking up, I see Drew standing in front of our ticket table. *Did he hear everything I just said?* I wonder. *¡Ay!* He gives me a grin, then pops a stick of bubblemint gum into his mouth. He offers a stick to me too, but I'm too embarrassed to take it.

"Howdy, Drew!" Bea says, tipping her cowgirl hat at him. "We're selling tickets to the Sadie Hawkins dance. Have you heard about it?"

Drew laughs. "Yeah, I might have heard a rumor. Henry said you asked him to go with you."

Bea nods, happily. "It's going to be super fun! Henry wants to dress up like a cactus, instead of a cowboy, just to be different."

Drew laughs again. "That sounds like something Hen would do."

Bea leans in. "What kind of costume are *you* planning to wear?" she asks Drew.

I give Bea a nudge with my elbow.

"Not sure," Drew replies. "But I'll take a cowboy hat." He pulls some money from his pocket.

"Just *one* hat?" Bea persists. "Some of the guys are buying *two* and giving the extra one to their *date*."

I give Bea another poke in the side.

"I'll just take one for now," Drew says. "I don't have a date yet."

"Really?" Bea says. "What a coincidence. *Vicka* doesn't have a — *ouch!*"

"*Hat*," I blurt out, giving Bea a dagger-sharp poke with my elbow. "She means I don't have a *hat* yet. Here, let me get one for you, Drew." Quickly, I jump up and reach for the top cowboy hat on the stack. But instead of grabbing it, I knock over the whole tower!

"Timber!" Drew shouts as cowboy hats fall and scatter like tumbleweeds across the floor! A moment later, Drew, Bea, and I start chasing down hats and restacking them.

Drew picks up the last two hats, puts one on his head, and holds the other one out to me. "You need a hat too, Vicka," he says. "My treat." Then he puts the hat into my hands.

"Um . . . er . . . thanks," I manage to say as he pays Bea for two hats.

"No problem. Happy trails!" he says, tipping his hat to Bea and me. Then he saunters over to the group of girls who bought tickets and hats earlier.

"Did you see that?" Bea says as we watch Drew talking with the girls. "He totally grinned when he gave you the hat!"

"So?" I say, putting the hat on. "He's *always* grinning. He's grinning right *now* at those other girls."

"But the grin he gave you wasn't ordinary," Bea says, matter-of-factly. "It was a . . . grin of hope. He wants you to ask him to the dance!"

I make a doubtful face at Bea.

"Grins don't lie," she tells me. "Ask him, Vicka. *Today.* Before it's too late!"

When I get home after school, I am still dateless for the dance. I wonder if any other girl has this unfortunate problem. My dream of dancing with my crush is fading into the sunset.

I trudge to my bedroom, drop my backpack on the floor, take off my cowgirl hat, and plop down on my bed. Poco hops up next to me as I pull a pack of bubblemint gum from my hoodie pocket. I found it under our ticket table in the Caf when Bea and I were packing up everything to take back to the office. Drew must have dropped it when he helped us pick up the hats I knocked over.

Instead of giving it back to him, I tucked it in my pocket and carried it around all afternoon. Is it stealing if you keep something your crush doesn't even know he lost?

Poco pokes his nose at my hand, sniffing the gum.

"No, Poco, it's not a doggie treat," I say, tucking the gum under my pillow. "It belongs to Drew. I'll give it back to him the next time I see him. By then he'll have a date to the dance. Everyone will, except me."

Poco whimpers, then wags his tail encouragingly. Sometimes I think my dog can understand what I'm saying. Maybe he's an enchanted pup, like the bear prince in Lucas's favorite folktale. On the outside Poco is a chihuahua, but on the inside he is my trusted friend.

I stroke Poco's fur as he snuggles in. "Maybe I'm enchanted too . . ." I say. "For all I know, I'm really a brave, confident girl trapped inside average, ordinary me. I wish I had a magic potion that would break the spell so everyone could see the me I am inside."

Poco noses my pillow and, a moment later, pulls the pack of gum out from underneath it. He drops it on my lap, then wags his tail proudly. "Yip-yip!" he barks.

"Thanks, Poco, but this is just gum, not a magic potion." Still, I unwrap a stick and start chewing, just in case.

Chapter 10

Saturday at the Park

The next morning, I pick up the package of Drew's gum I left on my dresser last night. It's crumpled and half empty now. I chewed two more sticks before I went to bed, hoping they would give me confidence for what I have to do today.

Tucking the gum in my pocket, I hop on my bike and head to the skate park. I didn't ask Bea to come with me because I know she has piano lessons. Besides, it feels like this is something I have to do on my own.

When I get to the skate park, I see Drew warming up on one of the ramps. Good. I was hoping he'd get here early. Only a few other kids have shown up so far. I drop my bike by the path, take the pack of gum from my pocket, and walk over to Drew. He's sitting on the ramp now, retying his shoelace.

"Hi, Drew," I say, stopping in front of the ramp.

Drew glances up, then does a double take. "Hey, Vicka!" he says, hopping down. "You came! But you're early. The demo doesn't start for another hour."

"I know," I reply. "But I wanted to catch you before Anne — I mean, before everyone else gets here." I hold out the pack of gum. "You dropped this in the Caf yesterday. I . . . um . . . didn't have a chance to give it back to you . . . so I thought I'd bring it to the park today. And . . . er . . . I might have chewed a few pieces."

Drew takes the gum from me. "Thanks," he says, tucking it in his pocket. "But you didn't have to bring it all the way over here."

"I know, but . . . actually . . . there's another reason I came," I reply.

"Oh, yeah?" Drew says. "Did you want to give skateboarding a try? I could teach you a trick or two before the demo."

"No, that's not it," I say. "I mean, I'd like to learn, but maybe another time. Right now, I just want to ask you a question. It's about the Sadie Hawkins dance."

Drew's eyebrows go up. "Oh!" he says. "Okay, shoot."

I take a deep breath. "It's just . . . I was wondering if you're going to it . . . the dance, I mean . . . or maybe you don't even want to . . . *I'm* going, but mostly I'll be helping in the chuck wagon . . . but not the whole time because . . . um . . . we're going to take turns . . . so . . . if you did want to go and don't mind getting your toes stepped on . . . um . . . maybe we could —?"

Just then, a loud horn honks behind us. We turn and see a shiny black pickup truck with cool orange flames painted on it pulling in next to the skate park. One of its tinted windows rolls down, and Annelise's bright, smiling face appears. She's wearing a pink cowgirl hat that's studded with sparkly gems. I can see her dad behind the steering wheel. He's wearing a cowboy hat too.

Annelise sees us and waves, then hops out of the truck. "Howdy, Drew!" she calls out over the country music that's blasting from the truck's speakers. "Have *I* got a surprise for you!!"

Curious kids head over to the fancy truck, checking it out, and talking to Annelise. I hear her tell them her dad borrowed the truck from a friend. Someone takes out a phone and starts snapping selfies in front of it. Annelise rushes over and grabs Drew by the arm, dragging him into one of the group shots.

I watch as Annelise plops her sparkly cowgirl hat on Drew's head, laughing as they take funny selfies together.

I like taking selfies with my friends as much as anyone. But my question to Drew is still hanging in the air, halfway asked, and completely unanswered. Soon, Annelise will whisk him away to the Lazy L where she'll ask him the same question. Only she'll get her answer there.

"Do you want to go to the riding stables with me after the demo?" I hear Annelise ask Drew.

Drew shrugs. "Sure, why not!"

"It's a date!" Annelise replies, giving Drew a high five.

Annelise's perfect plan is falling into place. My plan just fell apart.

I head back to my bike, tears burning in my eyes, my heart breaking into a zillion pieces. I'm not upset with Annelise or Drew. Why shouldn't they go to the dance together? She came up with a super fun way to ask him, and it's working.

The only person I'm upset with is me. I had tons of chances to ask Drew to the dance, and I let each one slip away. I know raising money for our school and collecting food for the local pantry is what the fundraiser is all about. But, right now, all I can think about is how unfortunately left out I feel.

I climb onto my bike and start pedaling up the hill. I have no idea where I'm going. If I go home, I'll spend the rest of the day sulking in my room, earbuds in and the door shut tight, feeling sorry for myself.

The hill is getting steeper now. This is where Bea and I usually get off our bikes and start pushing them the rest of the way up. But today, I keep pedaling, feeling my leg muscles burn like they're catching fire. It matches the burning in my eyes and the pain in my chest.

"I could . . . bike to . . . Java Jane's . . ." I huff and puff to myself as my bike wobbles with each push of the pedal. "When I get there . . . I'll text Bea . . . tell her to meet me . . . after piano lessons . . ."

Bea could help me drown my sorrows in an extra large hot chocolate and a whole plate of cookies. But would that really make me feel better about everything? Maybe for a little while but not forever. Besides, I know Bea is planning to watch Henry skate at the demo today.

I'm almost to the top of the hill now, and my legs are seriously complaining. I keep pushing against the pain, inching up and up and up, legs blazing like Annelise's pickup truck, hot tears trailing down my cheeks.

When I finally make it to the top of the hill, I stop, breathing hard and wincing against my cramping muscles. But as much as I hurt, a part of me actually feels better. My heart is pounding like a hammer against my chest. I guess it isn't broken, after all. In fact, it feels stronger than ever. I'm exhausted, but in a weird way, I feel stronger too.

As I coast down the other side of the hill, my legs smile gratefully. The breeze dries my tears. My heart makes a decision.

I'm not going to sulk in my room today. I won't drown my sorrows in sweets. I'm going to Abuela's house, I tell myself. *Maybe she needs help cutting her grass or weeding her flower garden this morning. Then this afternoon, I'll take Lucas and Poco to the park.*

I haven't done that in ages. Tonight, I'm getting Sofia to make popcorn with me. We'll tell everyone we're having a movie night. Maybe Bea and Jenny can come over too.

By the time I get to the bottom of the hill, I feel different. Not happy, exactly, but not broken either. As I start pedaling again, I realize my head feels clear for the first time in weeks. Like I finally cured myself of dance fever. I'm still unfortunately dateless for the dance, but that's okay. I have more important things to do.

Chapter 11

A Zillion Small Distractions

On Monday morning, Drew comes to school sporting the *#1 Skater* shades from Saturday's demo. He's also wearing a Lazy L lanyard around his neck. It's just like the one I got when I went horseback riding there.

A bunch of Drew's friends come up to him, slapping his back and giving him fist bumps. "You were sick at the park on Saturday, skater dude!" Henry tells Drew. Then he spies the lanyard Drew is wearing. "Are you as good at riding a horse as you are at riding a skateboard?"

Drew laughs. "Not a chance. My horse had a mind of its own. When I pulled on the right rein, the horse went *left*. When I pulled on the left rein, it went *right*. When we came to a mud puddle along the trail, it did a one-eighty, then took off into the bushes! Everyone was cracking up when it trotted onto the trail again with me swatting away bugs and branches." Drew pushes up the sleeves on his shirt to show everyone the scratches and bug bites on his arms.

"Are you sure the horse wasn't just trying to get away from Annelise?" Henry asks under his breath. All the guys snicker.

Drew cracks a grin. "Ah, she wasn't so bad," he says, pulling down his sleeves again. "The whole day was pretty fun, actually, and that truck her dad borrowed was seriously rad."

All week, Annelise and Drew kid around at school, talking about their funniest moments at the riding stables. When Annelise's friends bring up the dance, I hurry away not wanting to hear her gush about going with Drew. A couple times, I see them eating lunch together, and, yesterday, Annelise got Drew to help her and Will work on the backdrop for the photo booth. I saw them when I walked past the art room on my way to the gym. I've been helping decorate it during my study halls and after school. Everyone on the committee has been pitching in.

At first, I felt a twinge of jealousy when I saw Annelise and Drew together. But now it's Friday, and seeing them together doesn't bother me as much anymore. Before this week, asking someone to the dance seemed like the biggest deal in the world. But ever since I left the skate park on Saturday, I've been seeing things differently. With the pressure of asking Drew for a date off my shoulders, I feel a million times lighter and a lot more like me.

Annelise thinks bigger is better, and I suppose sometimes that's true. It's fun to plan a big event and get lots of people jazzed about coming to it. Plus, raising a lot of money for a worthy cause is never a bad thing.

But I think small is good too. Each day this week, there were a zillion small things that needed to get done so the fund-raiser can go off without a hitch tomorrow. I helped with half-a-zillion of them — everything from filling zippy bags with pioneer trail mix to sell at the chuck wagon, to making paper-chain garlands to decorate the gym, to painting posters for the game booths, to helping Principal Oates haul a van load of canned goods to the food pantry so we'd have room for more in our donation box.

It made me feel like I was shining from the inside out each time we completed a task. I can't wait until tomorrow when my family will see how all our hard work has paid off. I still wouldn't mind going to the dance, but popping popcorn and serving hot dogs isn't a bad way to spend the night, either. And the truth is, I'm probably not ready to go on a date yet. Maybe I will be when I'm older, but right now helping out and having fun with my friends is more important.

❀ ❀ ❀

"Ready to go, Calamity Jane?" Dad asks as I finish tying a red kerchief around my neck to match the red pom-poms that dangle from the brim of a sombrero I found in a trunk in Abuela's attic. It's fancier than the cowgirl hat I wore at the carnival, plus it matches the red ribbons Mom used when she braided my hair.

With my fringed vest, plaid shirt, and faded jeans, Dad must think I look like the legend-ary Calamity Jane, a frontierswoman who was super spunky and famous for her kindness to others. There was even a question about her on our last history test — which I aced, by the way. Yee-haw for me!

"Almost ready," I reply. "I just have to grab the bag of canned goods I'm bringing for our food pantry donation box."

Actually, we had to add a *second* box because the first one is overflowing with more food that kids and teachers have been bringing to school. It looks like Principal Oates will have to kiss a cow three times tonight!

At the carnival this afternoon, she declared this event to be one of the best fund-raisers our school has ever hosted. You should have seen the look on Sofia's face when everyone burst into applause. She floated from game booth to game booth for the rest of the day.

Dad gives me a big smile as I lug a grocery bag filled with cans and boxes of food to our front door. "Sofia, Mom, and Lucas just carried more donations out to the car," he says, taking the bag from me. "Everyone at your school is very generous! I can't wait to meet them at the dance!"

"I'll be helping in the food booth tonight, so I probably won't see much of you on the dance floor," I tell Dad.

"Well then, we better get a dance in right now!" Dad sets down the grocery bag.

I giggle as he takes my hand and gives me a spin. Waltzing around our entryway, Dad twirls me again and again. We take our bows, then it's off to the dance!

Chapter 12

Want to Dance?

"Stand back, dudes, or someone is gonna get hurt!" Henry calls out as he and Bea step into the gym lobby during a break between songs the DJ is playing. The gym and lobby are packed with cowgirls and cowboys.

Bea giggles and shakes her head at Henry as kids come up to him, pretending to poke themselves on the fake spikes that are sticking out from his cactus costume. Bea helped him attach a bunch of plastic soda straws to the green sweatsuit he's wearing. He even painted his face green! Bea is wearing a super cute skirt, gingham top and, of course, her cowgirl hat. Her hair is braided with red ribbons, just like mine!

I can't wait to hang out with her and Jenny later, but right now I'm too busy helping in the chuck wagon. Lots of kids are grabbing a bite to eat during the break in the music. So far, the dance is a huge success! Tons of kids are here, and everyone seems to be having a good time.

"Excuse me? We'd like some popcorn, please," I hear someone say as I scoop popcorn into paper bags. Glancing over my shoulder, I see Annelise waving a dollar bill at me. Will is standing next to her.

"Oh, hi, Vicka!" she says as I step up to the counter. "I didn't recognize you. Cute hat, by the way. We'd like some popcorn." She sets down her money and smiles at Will. "My treat."

I blink with surprise under the brim of my sombrero. *Why is Annelise buying Will popcorn?* I wonder. *Shouldn't she be buying it for Drew?* I glance around to see if he's with her.

"Um . . . I'd like that popcorn *today*, Vicka," Annelise says impatiently. "The break is almost over, and Will and I have some serious dancing to do!"

Will grins. His ears pink up under his cowboy hat.

I shake my head confused. "Um . . . sure . . . but . . . can I talk to you for a minute, Annelise?" I set two bags of popcorn on the counter. "Alone?"

Annelise sighs, like this is a big inconvenience. But she hands the popcorn to Will. "Meet me by the gym doors," she tells him. "Vicka needs me."

Will nods and works his way through the crowd. I tell one of the chaperones I'll be right back, then slip out of the chuck wagon and meet up with Annelise in a corner of the gym lobby.

"What is it, Vicka?" Annelise asks. "Do you want to thank me for coming up with such a great idea for the dance? No need. I already know that having a Sadie Hawkins turned this fund-raiser into a huge success. I'm sure they'll beg me to chair the committee next year."

I ignore Annelise's bragging and get right to the point. "Why are you hanging out with Will? Shouldn't you be dancing with your date?"

Annelise laughs. "Will *is* my date, Silly. I asked him to the dance a few days ago. He's quiet, but he's really nice. And he's even a better artist than me! We worked all week on painting the photo booth backdrop. Have you seen it? It looks awesome!"

"I haven't seen it yet," I say, still feeling confused. "What about your big plan to ask Drew to be your date?"

"I did ask him." Annelise shrugs. "What can I say? He turned me down. It wasn't like he was mean about it or anything. And we still had a great time at the riding stables."

I frown, more confused than ever. "Then why did he say no?"

"Because Henry told him someone else was planning to ask him, and he wanted to wait until she did." Annelise flicks back her long braided ponytail.

"Whoever she is, she must have chickened out or changed her mind, because I saw Drew hanging out with the other dateless boys in the gym." Annelise pauses and gives me a curious look. "Who did you ask to the dance, by the way?"

I fidget in my cowgirl boots. "Um . . . I decided to stick with the food booth tonight. I'm not much of a dancer."

Annelise makes a face. "None of you are. But who cares?" She looks across the lobby and catches Will's eye. He smiles and lifts a bag of popcorn to her. Turning back to me, she says, "Gotta go, Vicka. Have fun making cowboy grub. *I'm* going to dance!"

Annelise hurries over to Will. They disappear into the gym just as the DJ begins playing tunes again.

I wander around the crowded lobby, deep in thought. *Will is Annelise's date?! Drew turned her down because he was waiting for someone else to ask him. I'm the reason he doesn't have a date to the dance.*

"Look out, Vicka!" someone shouts.

I jump back just before crashing into a cow! Actually, it's a cute little calf being led on a leash by Alex and his grandparents. Kids come up to pet the calf as they lead it into the gym where Principal Oates will kiss it in front of the crowd later. But I'm feeling too bummed about being a chicken and ruining Drew's night to pay much attention to the sweet calf.

As I turn back to the chuck wagon, I crash into something for real.

Thwump!

"¡Uf!"

"Howdy, Vicka! Nice bumping into you."

I look up to see Drew smiling back at me.

"Oh, hi!" I say, straightening my sombrero. "Sorry! I wasn't watching where I was going. I have to get back to the chuck wagon. I'm helping out, serving hot dogs and popping popcorn and stuff."

Drew nods. "I saw you there, earlier. Need any help? My popcorn-popping skills are legendary."

I laugh a little. "Sure! We need all the help we can get." But then I duck my eyes, still feeling guilty about him waiting for me to ask him to the dance. Glancing up, I say, "I heard you don't have a date tonight. I meant to ask you to go with me to the dance, but then . . . I didn't. I'm sorry."

Drew shrugs. "That's okay. I'm not much of a dancer anyway."

I smile. "Me either!"

A minute later, Drew and I are dumping oil and kernels into the chuck wagon's popcorn machine. As it spins out perfectly popped kernels of corn, Drew puts a popcorn bag on his hand, like a puppet.

"Hello, little girl," he says out of the corner of his mouth as he works the puppet, like it's talking to me. "What's your name?"

I giggle at the squeaky voice Drew is using. "I am Victoria Torres," I reply. "Who are you?"

"Call me Poppy," Drew says, making the puppet talk in a cartoon voice. "Did you know I'm a great dancer, Victoria Torres? Here, I'll show you . . ." Drew makes the puppet dance around the chuck wagon, bumping into cupboards and chaperones, like it's wigging out in a mosh pit.

I'm laughing so hard, my eyes are tearing up! As I watch one of the chaperones do-si-do with the puppet and Drew, I can't help but feel a twinge of regret for not asking Drew to be my date. But it only lasts for a moment. After all, I'm hanging out with my crush, and we're definitely having a good time!

Principal Oates comes around to check on how we're doing. When we show her all the money in the chuck wagon's cash box, she says, "When I add this amount to the money we raised at the carnival this afternoon, plus the sales of hats and dance tickets, I'm sure we will exceed our goal! And that doesn't even take into consideration the overflowing food pantry donation boxes!" She smiles at Drew and me. "Looks like I better pucker up. In a few minutes, I'll be giving a cow a very *big* kiss!"

We laugh as our principal takes out a tube of bright red lipstick and puts some on.

"You two better get out on the dance floor," Principal Oates says, tucking the lipstick back in her handbag. "I'll take your place in the chuck wagon. It's almost time for the Mexican Hat Dance!"

"It is?!" I exclaim. "I'm supposed to help my family lead that!"

"Better hurry then," our principal says.

I turn to Drew. "Um . . . do you want to . . . do you want to dance with me?"

A smile spreads across Drew's face. He tosses aside the puppet. "Sure!" he says. "I thought you'd never ask."

Dashing out of the chuck wagon, Drew grabs my hand and we race into the gym, zigzagging our way through the crowd. Sofia sees us and waves us over to the photo booth. Lucas is there, helping her take pictures of the dancers. As Drew and I collapse onto a hay bale, out of breath and laughing, Lucas gives us two giant foam cowboy hats to wear, then makes silly faces at us while Sofia snaps our picture.

A moment later, the DJ's music stops, and everyone turns to look as my parents enter the gym wearing beautiful costumes! Mom's dress is super colorful with a wide ruffled skirt. When she holds out the edges of the skirt, it looks like a beautiful fan. Dad's vest is black with silver trim. It matches the wide sombrero on his head! They look so great!

Dad's band joins them on the gym stage. They start getting ready to play while Mom and Dad step up to a microphone, greeting everyone.

"The Hat Dance is a traditional folk dance which has been performed for many years," Mom explains to the crowd. "It's so popular, it became the national dance of Mexico! Mr. Torres and I are wearing traditional costumes that once belonged to his grand-parents. We'll demonstrate the dance for you. Then our daughters, Sofia and Victoria, and our son, Lucas, will help us teach you some of the steps!"

As the band plays, Mom and Dad do a fancy version of the Hat Dance. They totally rock! Everyone claps like crazy as they take their bows.

"Now it's your turn," Mom announces. "Grab a partner!"

"That's our cue," Sofia says, setting down her camera and taking Lucas by the hand. "Come on you two!" she calls over her shoulder to Drew and me as she and Lucas hurry up to the stage.

I hesitate, but then I grab Drew's hand. We take off too. Before I know it, I'm on the stage of my school gym, dancing with my crush!

As soon as the dance comes to an end, we take our bows, and Alex's grandparents parade the calf on stage. Principal Oates comes forward and, without any hesitation, plants three big, red kisses on the calf's speckled nose! The crowd goes wild!

As they parade the calf off stage again, Dad joins the band to play another jazzy tune, while Mom, Sofia, and Lucas dance along.

"Drewster! Vicka!" a husky green cactus calls to us from the dance floor. "Get down here!" Henry and Bea wave to Drew and me.

A moment later, we hop down from the stage and start dancing like crazy with Henry and Bea in the middle of the crowd. Jenny and Sam are there too. Soon Annelise and Will bop over and join our circle. None of us are very good dancers, but like Annelise says, who cares? It's impossible not to shine when you are dancing with your friends!

About the Author

Julie Bowe lives in Mondovi, Wisconsin, where she writes popular books for children, including *My Last Best Friend*, which won the Paterson Prize for Books for Young People and was a Barnes & Noble 2010 Summer Reading Program book. In addition to writing for kids, she loves visiting with them at schools, libraries, conferences, and book festivals throughout the year.

Glossary

bribe (BRIBE)—to persuade someone to do something by offering them money or a gift

chuck wagon (CHUHK WAG-uhn)—a covered wagon or truck that serves as a portable kitchen

compromise (KAHM-pruh-myz)—to reach an agreement that is not exactly what either side wants in order to make a decision

crave (KRAVE)—to want something very much

exceed (ik-SEED)—to do bigger or better than something else

garland (GAR-luhnd)—a rope made from leaves, flowers, or other items

gingham (GING-uhm)—lightweight cotton cloth with a checked pattern

grimace (GIM-is)—a facial expression that usually expresses a negative reaction

PTO (PEE TEE OH)—stands for Parent Teacher Organization, a group of teachers, parents, and community members who work together to help and support a school

publicity (pub-BLIS-i-tee)—information about a person or an event that is given out to get the public's attention or approval

saunter (SAWN-tur)—to walk in a slow, leisurely, or casual way

surpass (sur-PAS)—to be better, greater, or stronger than another person or thing

tentative (TEN-tuh-tiv)—unsure or not confident

Time to Talk

Questions for you and your friends

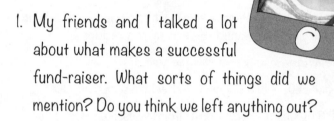

1. My friends and I talked a lot about what makes a successful fund-raiser. What sorts of things did we mention? Do you think we left anything out?

2. Even though I didn't want to be the one to do it, I had to talk to Annelise and get her to change her mind about the fund-raiser. In what ways did we compromise? Why do you think it's a good idea to meet someone halfway? Can you think of a time you've had to reach a compromise with someone?

3. Were you surprised that I never got around to asking Drew to the dance? Explain your answer. Would you have asked your crush? Why or why not?

Just for You

Writing prompts for your journal

1. It was difficult to find a theme for the fund-raiser that we could all agree on. It had to be a theme that students and community members could all enjoy. Can you think of any other themes besides Wild West that might have worked?

2. Plan out what your ideal fund-raiser carnival would be like. What theme would it have? What sort of food would you serve and games would you play? What would the money you raise go toward?

3. I spent day after day freaking out about asking Drew to the dance even though I had a plan, and Bea kept telling me he would say yes. I started to have nightmares, and I wasn't acting like myself. In the end, I realized that it wasn't that big of a deal. Have you ever made a situation bigger than it needed to be? Write about it.

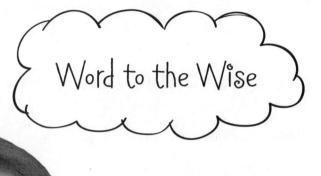

Word to the Wise

The idea of a school dance can make you smile, sweat, or both! Even though finding a date for a dance can be scary, the dance itself should be lots of fun. After my first big dance, I have a few ideas on how to make sure dances are 100% awesome.

Make your next dance the best ever!

Don't get wrapped up in finding a date for the dance. It's okay if you don't have one. You can still have tons of fun with your friends and family.

Always bring your best attitude. If you expect to have a bad time, you probably will. But if you plan on having fun, you'll have a blast.

Never bring your drama to the dance floor. Dances are for having fun with your friends and family, not confronting people or making a scene.

Confidence! It's important to have confidence on the dance floor. My friends and I aren't very good dancers, but we danced and had lots of fun anyway!

Enjoy yourself! Whether you're planning the dance or you're on the dance floor, it's important to have fun.

Cooking Corner

You read a lot about my time making popcorn (with Drew!), so I bet you wouldn't mind some popcorn of your own right now! Popcorn is a pretty basic snack, but there are a lot of fun ways you can make it special. This is one of my favorites!

WHITE-CHOCOLATE POPCORN

INGREDIENTS

2 bags microwave popcorn

¾ cup corn syrup

½ bag marshmallows

1 bag white chocolate chips

3 Tbsp butter

Find out more about Victoria's unfortunately average life, plus get cool downloads and more at www.capstonekids.com

(Fortunately, it's all fun!)

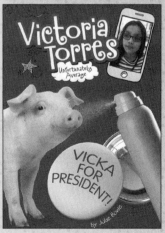

Victoria Torres

Unfortunately Average

Always looking
for her way to shine!

Victoria Torres
Unfortunately Average

CURVEBALL

by Julie Bowe

It's summertime and that means softball season! Victoria Torres is joining up with some of her friends to play coed softball on a city-league team coached by none other than her dad. As an experienced pitcher, Vicka thinks this is her chance to shine on the mound. But her dad has different plans. He wants her and her strong arm in centerfield, but Victoria hates being stuck in the outfield! How will she deal with this curveball?

EQUIPMENT

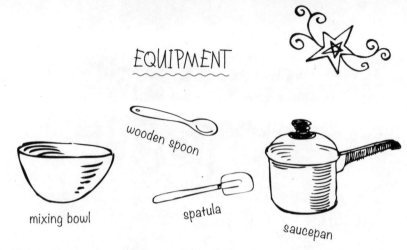

wooden spoon

mixing bowl

spatula

saucepan

1. Pop your popcorn and put it in a large bowl.

2. Melt the butter in the saucepan over medium heat. Stirring, add the corn syrup, marshmallows, and white chocolate, and bring to a boil.

3. Add the marshmallow mixture into the popcorn, and stir so that all of the popcorn and chocolate candy is coated.

4. With the rubber spatula, spread the popcorn out on waxed paper. Let cool.

MIX-IT-UP IDEAS

· Mix in sprinkles to make the popcorn extra festive! I think the sprinkles look like little pieces of confetti. It's great for parties.

· Use only certain colored chocolate candies to stick with a theme. If you're having a holiday party, use red and green candies. If it's around Valentine's Day, mix in red and pink!

· Mix 1 cup chocolate candy pieces with the popcorn in step 1. Or try it with crushed-up chocolate cream-filled cookies. It's a fun twist on the cookies-and-cream classic!